Three dark-robed ghouls crouched fa ▊▊▊ w, their eyes blank in the firelight. She might have been moved to pity for these former tradesmen or farmers if there had been any humanity left in them, but these were only bodies with lightless eyes and a hunger for blood. And even as she uneasily shifted the knife in her hand, their slavering mouths gaped to reveal terrifying fangs and the things moved forward to surround her.

Shadow reached behind her into the fire and pulled out a flaming table leg. Then she lunged forward, knife in one hand, torch in the other. A blink of white, shocked eyes, and one ghoul beat the air, his garment flaming, while another shuddered backward, blood pouring from his gut.

In her attack, Shadow had left the protection of the fire, and now the third ghoul leaped at her, hands reaching for her shoulders and teeth positioned to rip out her throat. The sheer weight of him bore her to the ground. Her wrist struck the dirt floor and the torch fell from her grasp. The knife remained, but the fiend had her pinned. His white eyes seemed to bore into hers, pulling, pulling, as though to suck out her insides. And then she felt the cold, the seeping fog within her mind. This nightmare creature was taking her soul for the Graylord. . . .

SHADOWLIGHT
JACKIE HYMAN

DAW BOOKS, INC.
DONALD A. WOLLHEIM, PUBLISHER

1633 Broadway, New York, NY 10019

DAW Book Collectors No. 802.

First Printing, December 1989

1 2 3 4 5 6 7 8 9

PRINTED IN THE U.S.A.

For Kurt

Chapter One

Shadow pressed herself flat against the slate roof, watching through a chink in the gutter as the bloodcat hunted her.

Its sightless eyes indifferent to the rain-clouded midday darkness, the wine-colored beast scoured the alley, from time to time lifting its wedge-shaped head to sniff the air. This was a larger one than most, its shoulders perhaps as high as her hips. Its raspy breathing echoed from the stones, the reverberations probing each rough crevice and contour.

All this, she reflected bitterly, and the Radiants had spotted her before she could steal the keys to the prison that held Nle. In trying to rescue her friend, she had revealed her existence, when after all these years the Radiant leader, Hakin, must have thought her dead.

And Hakin surely wanted her dead. This ancient land could not belong to them both. While Shadow lived, however degraded and hunted, she would never forget that she sprang from the old race of her mother and, on her father's side, from the Radiants who had overpowered and banished them.

But her thoughts now must be of finding refuge,

the only one possible at this moment—the Den of
Ashi. Packed with the dregs of Ad-Omaq, it was
dangerous, especially for one who had no friends.
And she'd had none since the capture of Dorf and
Nle. But there she might at least have a chance of
survival.

Below Shadow, the three hooded Radiants clus-
tered to one side, murmuring the chant of light-
giving to clear the clouded eyes of the bloodcat.
Shadow had never seen this done before, yet she
knew from the cat's sudden rigidity the exact moment when the vision came, and followed from its
movements how its sight flickered and beat against
the darkness.

Fools. Worshipers of the light, masters of its many
forms, the Radiants couldn't see its power to confuse. There was a saying in the streets of Ad-Omaq:
When the bloodcat sees, it is most blind. Apparently
the Radiants had never heard that bit of underworld
wisdom.

The adage proved true. Distracted by its newfound
vision, the bloodcat failed to note the whisper of
cloth-bound feet as Shadow slunk across the roof.

An edge of rain knifed through her thin ankle-tied
robe as she skimmed down a drainpipe. The storm
was a bit of good fortune. Even a ring-babble knew
bloodcats couldn't sense in a downpour. It bought
time for her to seek the Den.

But it might also drive the Radiants to use the
full-light, splashing illumination over the filthy
sneakways of Ad-Omaq like white paint on a grave.
She must find a hiding place before then.

Shadow skittered across a rubbish-strewn square,
one like a thousand others in this maze of a city. In
the rain, the dirt was already churning to mud and

writhing with lyworms in search of rotting carrion. Filth splattered against her coarse garments.

Drawing the tattered scarf tighter over the small horns that marked her as an outlaw of the old race, she merged into a corner and sent her mind flicking over the backways of the city. She'd spent the past dozen years dodging and thieving in this dark walled tangle, and knew it well. But sometimes stones shifted in the murk, and cracks opened and closed in the gutters, not always by chance.

The way to the Den of Ashi was forever shifting, and it would take all Shadow's city-sense to find it now. And all her courage.

It was not a place she would willingly go to under normal circumstances. The Den was home to the fugitives of the city, the robber-murderers, those whoremasters stupid enough to have enslaved Highborn women, and horned people of the old race, condemned because the Radiants feared they might have inherited unpredictable powers. The putrid charm of the place lay in its secrecy, sprawling tuberlike deep beneath the Citadel itself. They joked in that asylum that it was the only place in the city from which one must travel upward to reach the Radiants' dungeons.

There, in the most rotten stench-hole in the city, Shadow might find a perverse kind of safety. It was too dangerous to leave the city; and she must reach Nle before he could be handed over to the grayvers as tribute.

She settled her pack against her shoulders, which were accustomed to the weight of always carrying her few possessions with her. At least the rain was slacking. Shadow scanned the streetstones for some newly devised crack that might open into the abandoned sewers, which led to the Den of Ashi.

So absorbed was she in her seeking, Shadow almost walked directly into an Enforcer.

The squat, heavy-jowled guard and the small, sharp-featured girl gaped at each other for a moment. Shadow choked back her panic. He might not recognize her as a fugitive; in the dark, she looked much like any other girl. She nodded indifferently, as though she had nothing to fear, and started past.

He eyed her pack. "Got your house with you, eh?"

The homeless were subject to enslavement, so Shadow shook her head. "Odds and ends for juggling." She touched the knife hidden within her robe. She would not spill blood without good reason, but she would waste no pity on an Enforcer, either. Not when she'd seen the pleasure they took in tormenting the peasants who crowded into the city, desperate to escape the ghouls.

He was peering too closely at her eyes. She executed a ragged cartwheel sideways, wishing she'd spent more time practicing the tricks Nle had shown her.

"An acrobat? That doesn't prove anything." He confronted her again, his grin oily with appetite. "A street-sleeper, I'll bet. Make you a deal, girl. Give me my pleasure, and I might let you go afterward."

He reached for her and Shadow jerked away angrily. At that moment the full-light came, the brilliant glare slashing through the streets of Ad-Omaq, opening up the city as a man might turn out his pockets. Revealing the glint of yellow in her eyes that should belong only to a Radiant.

"Hey!" The Enforcer grabbed for her, careless,

fooled by her size and youth. "Something strange about you."

A quick, practiced thrust and his words ended in a death gurgle. Shadow jerked out the thin blade and replaced it in her belt. At another time, she would have searched the man for his Radiant-made light-weapons, but not with the city shining like midsummer.

Guttural voices rasped overhead. Heavy cloths lifted from window openings. Rarely now did the ordinary people venture out except from necessity, but this phenomenon drew them past their caution. As the Radiants had planned, the city was full of eyes and ears.

Running, her breath coming hard, Shadow tried one street, then another; she knew each intimately, but there was no predicting where a gap might open in the pavement. A woman leaned out overhead, loudly demanding to know what Shadow was doing, the shrill voice echoing until there was no telling who might notice.

She had to find the way, and quickly. Shadow closed her eyes against the light, summoning. This was her small trick, one even the Radiants didn't know, but one she used sparingly, for it drained her strength.

With an effort, she found a vision of the route. Opening her eyes and battling shakiness, Shadow dragged herself down the street and around a corner. The alley broke off as she'd foreseen and at the end, by the crumbling foundation of an old wall, she spied a gap barely wide enough for her slender body. Those who lived their lives in the Den of Ashi did not make it easy for visitors to find them.

The dimness of the ancient sewers seemed sooth-ingly cool to Shadow's eyes after the full-light. She stumbled, panting, and nearly lost her balance. It was always wearying to use her special talent. There hadn't been much need for the clarity until now, except sometimes to spy weapons on one who claimed to be a friend.

Her mother, Mera, had said the clarity might develop as Shadow grew, might strengthen with use into something deep and many-faceted. She had said more, much of which Shadow scarcely remembered; that gifts grew best nearest their source, and that the old race had sprung from the mountains where Shadow was born. But here in the city, skill with a knife meant more than all the old talents combined.

Shadow took a deep breath. She must not linger near the surface, where the cat might smell her blood. Folding her scarf away, she slogged forward through the foul air. Although the sewers were no longer used since neglect had allowed the grates to clog, they trickled with runoff from the rain, and here and there a munt or a ring-babble had crawled inside and died. As her eyes adjusted to the faint glow seeping in, Shadow saw one furred munt-shape stir as if alive, but from the odd, rough movements she knew it was only a pack of lyworms, fighting over their food.

She picked her way carefully. The downward angle, the wetness and the lack of handholds made the going slippery, and the scant illumination faded to almost nothing. Yet she dared not weaken herself further by using the clarity again. Shadow checked the hilt of her knife, assuring herself that it was still in place. It would be little use, though, against anyone less bungling than that Enforcer.

Would the Radiants guess she had entered the sewers? Nle had taught her that they and their Enforcers ignored the ancient slopways. But this time could be different. She was not an ordinary fugitive.

Burned into Shadow's memory was the bitter triumph in Hakin's eyes at the execution of the horned woman Mera, nearly twelve years before. The victim had stood proudly erect, refusing to weep as the Radiants scorched her with their light. But Shadow had wept, a child alone, longing for the wise edge of Mera's voice and the healing touch of her work-roughened hands. Even now, the remembered pain clouded her eyes.

Stretching her shoulders against the weight of the pack, she brushed one hand against the top of her head in an instinctive gesture for good luck. Her horns were small ones, easily hidden beneath the scarf.

Survivors of the old race were feared and hated for their unpredictable powers and their refusal to concede the Radiants' supremacy. Her mother's blood in her alone would have made her despised, even had she not inherited the yellow eyes of her father, Taav.

He had been the leader of the Radiants, the highest of the adepts. How furious Hakin must have been to learn that her husband had betrayed her with a horned woman and fathered a bastard, a half-sister and potential rival to her daughter Briala. Nor would Hakin have forgiven him for the risk of mingling his gifts with Mera's to produce a child of unknown powers.

Unknown powers. Well, Shadow supposed the range of her clarity was still unknown. And she had also inherited a bond to this land of her ancestors, and a hatred for those who misused it. Instinctively, she blamed the Radiants for the growing power of the grayvers. Surely a true leader would have found a way to fight the wraiths from the mountains and not been so quick to accommodate their inhuman appetites.

As she crept on through the sewers, Shadow's city-sense said she was passing under the doors of the Citadel. That sanctum of the Radiants rose pearl-white atop the dingy hillside labyrinth of Ad-Omaq, cliff-edged above the Omaq River.

Few of the wretches who battled their lives away in the killing streets knew that the city of Ad-Omaq had begun as a beacon of light, built five centuries before at the command of the Council which then ruled from the Western capital of Ad-Son, across the ocean. Shadow had learned from her father how, under Council orders, the city with the Citadel at its peak sprang up in the days when Omaq was a land of farms and villages ruled by the Magedom of Kir. The purpose was to entice Radiants from their scattered homes to work together, to refine their gift of narrowing light, to discover new ways of healing and of creating wonders. But they had been corrupted instead, turning to domination, hedonism and war, and in the course of time they'd reduced most of Ad-Omaq to a rotting heap of living rubbish.

Shadow's reflections sheered off as she caught a whiff of body odor bespeaking the nearness of the Den of Ashi.

She paused to consider her course. Her nickname derived from her skill at passing about the city unnoticed, and even here she had entered a time or two without attracting the attention of the watchers at the door. Or she might go boldly in, swaggering a little, catching the gleam of firelight on yellow eyes. Her strangeness, coupled with a reputation for having light fingers and a ready knife, had earned her a grudging measure of respect in these parts.

That suited her best. Slyness was enough for a brief visit; to last here, she must be bold. That way, her chances of surviving might reach fifty-fifty, on a good day.

Shadow shook out the long black hair to reveal her horns and strode to the guard. Before he could speak, she whipped out her knife.

From the gloom a second man coalesced, toothless and cold-eyed; then a third, half his face eaten away by acid. Watching the knife, willing her to attack. Wanting an excuse to kill her.

Shadow elevated the knife, the point against one forefinger, turning it so that all might see the dark stain on the blade. "Enforcer's blood," she said.

Reluctantly the toothless man uttered a laugh, stinking with foul breath, and stepped aside to let her pass.

Shadow made her way through a drift of onlookers to one of the battered tables. She looked up to order a drink and found Ashi already at hand, the short one-eyed innkeeper holding out a glass of translucent orange-tinted brew.

"I haven't asked for anything."

"Drink. You are my guest."

Around her, conversations dimmed. A head turned, then another.

Ashi must know she came as a fugitive, not a visitor; he had his own secret passageways into the storehouses of the Citadel, it was rumored, and his own spies. Here in his hideout he ruled with absolute power. The weak might be slain at the entrance, but the cunning and the strong who passed within still faced this final death-test at the hands of Ashi.

Shadow knew he had already passed judgment; the answer was in the drink.

She took the glass. It might hold pure finot, which lifted the spirits without dulling the senses, or it might be laced with aka, the venom of the aka-serpent. In either case, she must not show fear, must not refuse to drink. She had seen a man torn apart by his own companions for such cravenness.

Raising the glass in salute, she brought it to her lips and swallowed its contents in one long gulp. All eyes were fixed on her, waiting. Beyond Ashi, the fire leaped in its pit, casting blood-red brilliance over the assembly.

A sense of well-being pervaded Shadow. To feel so in this place could only mean the drink had been finot. She returned the glass to Ashi. "Another." He brought it, and she paid with an old coin minted in Kir.

Shadow relaxed slightly, enjoying the heat of the fire. It was amusing to think that, high above, the smoke vented itself through a crevice in the baths and was claimed by the Radiants to derive from magical origins.

She hadn't been here for months. The place was larger than she remembered, the roof double a man's height, extending far and tapering at the edges into rootlike channels where the denizens slept, and whored, and murdered each other.

Her coins were well distributed about her clothing, so a sneak thief would find only a small part of them in any one place. But they would not last long; Ashi charged well for his services. And one dared not sleep without companions to stand guard. Shadow must make a new life here if she were to survive, yet her thoughts were still of Nle and of the need to rescue him.

And then, as always, to watch the ways of the Radiants. To seek a chink in their power, however long it might take her.

In repose, Shadow's mind replayed the events of the past few weeks, since her friends had been captured.

As she had done several times before to spy on the Radiants, she had crept into the Citadel through the vents, an entrance she had discovered years ago by using the clarity. She had located Dorf and Nle in their cells deep underground, but had found no way to release them.

Two weeks ago, while she watched in frustration and rage, Dorf had been taken as tribute to the grayvers. Seeing that she must risk discovery by Hakin if she were to save Nle, Shadow had climbed upward, watching the levels where Radiants lived and worked, hoping for a chance to steal a key that might free her friend. Finally, today, she had thought she might have that chance.

She had been spying at the top of the Citadel, where the Radiant adepts ruled from high above Ad-Omaq. Through a grate she had peered into Hakin's room, watching the Radiant leader converse with her daughter Briala. Keys dangled from Hakin's pocket, and Shadow's hand tightened about her hook as she waited, hoping to snare them while the woman's attention was absorbed elsewhere.

The pair were arguing. Unable to make her move until Briala left, Shadow listened to her half-sister quarrel with Taav's widow.

"Are you mad?" the girl was saying. The fury in her face made her look older than Shadow, although they were almost the same age. "An alliance with Kir? That means surrender!"

"We must be rid of the grayvers." Hakin ran nervous fingers through her hair. "It's not worth it."

"It's worth anything!"

An alliance with Kir? Shadow knew Omaq had quarreled with the neighboring country of Kir long ago. Then, a half-dozen years back, the Mage of Kir had gone further, shutting the forest paths to the caravans that once passed from the port of Ad-Kir to the city of Ad-Omaq. But despite the Mage's legendary powers, which he might use to subjugate Omaq if given the opportunity, surely an alliance with him was preferable to the depredations of the grayvers.

Like the other dwellers in Ad-Omaq, Shadow knew little about these invaders from the mountains. Creatures of myth, almost forgotten after more than a millennium, they had suddenly returned in recent years. Creatures of fog and darkness, they sucked the soul from a man and left him an empty, blood-craving ghoul.

The effects of the grayvers' resurgence, and of the ghouls they had created, were unmistakable: the desolation of the land, the deaths of hundreds of peasants and the routing of the others. Instead of fighting, the Radiants maintained an uneasy truce by yielding up prisoners each month as tribute. As they had done with Dorf. And would do with Nle, if Shadow did not free him.

"We must have more blast-powder to fight the grayvers at their source." Hakin glared at her daughter. "We can only get it with Kir's cooperation. And we will get it. We must get it." She was muttering half to herself. "I must be rid of the Gray Ones."

Briala's yellow eyes glimmered beneath her dark

hair. "You think of no one but yourself. Not of me; no, never of me. Coward!"

Before the girl could react, Hakin's hand slapped across her cheek hard enough to bring tears. It was at that moment that Hakin caught the gleam of yellow pupils through the grating. At first, she might have thought herself spied upon by another Radiant; but as Shadow scrambled downward and escaped from the vents she was seen, and her strong resemblance to Briala left no doubt that she was the long-vanished daughter of Taav and Mera.

Now, biding her time in the Den of Ashi, Shadow turned the conversation over in her mind. Blast-powder. Taav had mentioned it once, when Shadow was a child, and then had fallen silent. So blast-powder was a tool of the Mage of Kir.

Why should Briala prefer the grayvers to him? The Mage—for Taav had met him once and described him—was only a man, although a man possessed of great powers and cunning. Stories were told of him in the streets of Ad-Omaq, of how he created beasts from air and summoned armies with the wave of an arm; but this was surely fable, or he would have conquered Omaq long ago.

As for the grayvers, had they anything to do with the fact that, for the past ten years, Hakin alone of all her caste had not aged? Or that suddenly, in middle age, her handsome looks had metamorphosed into fascinating beauty? Or that she had succeeded to her late husband's post as leader with no apparent opposition? Perhaps in exchange for tribute, the grayvers had yielded something more than a promise not to attack the city.

Shadow drew her thoughts back to the present as a thin man, his face welted with scars, took a seat and ordered more finot for them both. From various parts of the crowd, men were drifting her way. Seeking alliances, perhaps. Or planning to pass themselves off as friends, then rape and kill as she slept. She must find allies, must trade as little as possible for their protection. "Waiting for friends?" the thin man asked.

"Perhaps."

A third chair scraped forward at the table. This man she knew slightly: Argen, leader of his own gang. He was a hard outlaw, but she had never seen him commit an act of wanton cruelty. Argen tilted back in the wooden chair, regarding her inscrutably. Large-barreled, broad-boned, he gave the impression of lazy indifference, but Shadow knew how quick and deadly he could be.

"I wondered how long before you joined us, Yellow-eyes." He took the thin man's finot for his own. The man glared and departed. Others who had edged toward them stopped, and waited. "I heard Dorf went in the last tribute. And Nle lies in the dungeon, until his turn."

"Not if I . . ." She stopped herself, and quoted the saying, "Friends who are gone are friends no more."

"A cripple and a half-wit. How were they caught?"

"Bad luck." Despite his shattered leg, Nle was a master at surviving in the city. And Dorf might lack brains, but he was strong enough to defend himself. "Four Enforcers caught them with their pockets full of gems from a Highborn house."

"So the grayvers gain two more ghouls, and Ad-Omaq loses two more thieves. But they didn't catch you. You're a clever one, Yellow-eyes."

Shadow sipped at the brew and kept silent.

"You can't stay here alone," said Argen.

"I have need of new friends." It was a concession to admit even that much, but Shadow had quickly weighed Argen against the other men lingering nearby, and she knew he was the least treacherous.

"One must have something to trade." Argen regarded her, not with the greedy expression of the Enforcer, yet it was the same look. He reached one hand across the table, to her cheek. She allowed the touch.

"You haven't been taken yet, have you?" he said.

"No."

His breath quickened. "We need a woman."

"I will not serve a gang."

He was caught. The air lay heavy with his lust. Now he would agree to anything; later might come disavowal. Later was later. "Mine alone, then."

Shadow nodded and rose, following him. She had seen the couplings in the Street of Lost Women, and felt disgust. But she knew her choices. It might even be possible, later, to persuade Argen to help her free her friend. Nle knew every quirk of the city, and would be useful to him.

Barely at the edge of the crowd, Argen seized her, his hands probing, his scent thick and musky. Shadow willed herself to yield, softening her muscles, choking back the instinct to protect herself with a knife-thrust.

And then—light! Flashing through the den, glaring away the darkness in a great rush. Argen spun around to face the room, leaving Shadow free.

Day-brightness invaded the bowels of the earth, revealing Ashi's hole in all its degradation, the pockmarked faces, disease-bulged eyes. Some of the occupants cried out against brilliance such as they had not seen for years, hands attempting to hide their damning horns—one man had dozens, covering his entire head. Most drew weapons: daggers, axes, maces, handbows, cudgels and slings.

Shadow did not need the clarity to interpret what had happened. The Radiants had found the Den of Ashi, and they were looking for her.

Amid the uproar, she slipped unnoticed farther to the back of the chamber, where caverns funneled into the ancient sewers. Then the eerie, reverberating wail of the bloodcat doused the room with silence, a treacherous hush that waited to betray any movement.

"We've long known such a slime-hole as this existed, but we never troubled to find it before." It was a woman who spoke, vibrant and strong, and although her face was hidden behind the massed bodies, her voice marked her unmistakably. So Hakin herself had come, meaning at last to destroy her husband's bastard.

A man spoke; it was the Radiant beside Hakin. "Put away your weapons. It would be a small matter for us to obliterate the lot of you."

Everyone knew this was true, but the words were ill-chosen. Several in the crowd snarled defiances at this attempt to shame them. Covered by the noise, Shadow took a few steps backward. The bloodcat keened again. It couldn't find her scent amid all this fetor, but it knew her sound. She halted.

Hakin resumed her speech. "We've chosen to tolerate this vile place until now, because you prey upon each other. But now you welcome our enemy, a girl of perverted birth who has dared to spy upon the Radiants. She is named Mera-ti, child of Mera. Yield her to us, and this time we leave you unmolested."

There could be no mistaking who was meant, not

after Shadow's brazen entrance. Heads turned, fingers pointed, harsh voices lifted. Not Argen's; in one sharp moment, she saw him staring with hands clenched, and knew he would have helped her, if he could.

Shadow ran. The scream of the bloodcat licked after her, hoarse with frustration as it struggled to penetrate the crowded den. Her only advantage was her head start, and that dwindled rapidly as she lurched along the sewers, once falling so that her hands pressed into the viscous ooze. It was a strain to see in the grotesque light that crooked through the sewers sent by the Radiants behind her. She couldn't go on running blindly. She must make a plan. Must go—where? There was only one possibility, not of escape but of defiance. The sewers emptied into the Omaq River. It was a death plunge from the walls, but at least it was a clean one.

As she ran, stumbled, slogged forward, Shadow heard the beast gaining. The Radiants likely trailed some distance behind, for their light flickered only feebly here. At any moment she might feel the thing's searing breath upon her neck, and the jagged teeth rending down her back as she had seen one attack a boy who stole a chalice from the Citadel.

The finot helped clear her panic and she drew on the clarity. Ashi had a nasty secret that Nle had shown her once; there, it was down that corridor and a twist to the right.

Another dash brought her to the junction of two passages marked by a pile of bones and rotten cloth jutting from the muck. It was no accident so many had died here; but their misfortune might prove to be her luck.

A sharp jog to the left and she made a desperate

lunge upward. In the semi-darkness, Shadow's mud-stiffened hands clamped desperately on the rods Ashi had mounted overhead, the shock of the leap jarring through her shoulders and nearly knocking her loose.

With every dram of strength in her muscles, Shadow furled her body and kicked at a second rod. Somehow she managed to catch the bar with one foot and anchor her legs over it. Panting, she hung against the roof, listening to the deadly murmur in the mud below.

The bloodcat shrieked with joy as it splayed around the corner and leaped at its prey. The razor claws tore across the side of Shadow's shoulder with a searing wrench. She shuddered and tightened her grip on the rod.

The dimness in the sewers cleared a little—sign of the Radiants' nearing—and she watched the beast land, its haunches tensing for the death leap. In the slime, something coiled.

The bloodcat's howl of anguish rocked the caverns and nearly tore Shadow from her perch. The aka-serpent killed with its tongue, stabbing into the furred belly of the creature, sending its fiery poison to the heart.

This was the trap Ashi had laid for the unwary, not out of malice but because the only way to obtain the poison was from the bodies of victims. To what curious ends would he put poison extracted from a bloodcat?

"Bloodcat!" It was the echo of a Radiant's call, distant but clearly heading this way. Soon the light would seek Shadow out, and against their fire she had no weapon.

She dropped her feet and dangled by her hands, clenching her teeth against the pain in her shoulder.

She swung, building up speed, and then loosed the rods, flinging herself forward and narrowly clearing the pit. Before an Enforcer crippled him, Nle had been a street acrobat, and he had taught Shadow what he could.

One fork in the junction, she knew, led back to the city; she took the other. It sloped down, a good sign, and the air stirred, a shade less fetid.

Behind her, the Radiants had discovered the pit and the bloodcat, their illumination no doubt warning them in time to avoid the writhing serpents. A guttural curse echoed down the tunnel. It was a pleasure, even if a slight one, to distress Hakin, who hand-raised the beasts herself.

Shadow's breath came shallow and fast as she ran. She skidded several times, and her stiffening shoulder pained her. The Radiants made faster progress, for they had their light as guide.

The angle of descent steepened, and Shadow slid down the final passageway, catching herself at the raw-edged opening by bracing against the sides. In blew the sweet dark wind, cold and rain-laced but fresh with the scent of the living world. Far below, Shadow heard the roiling rush of the Omaq River. Then a wash of light framed her against the night, hair falling loose to reveal the nubs on either side of her head.

She turned, and found herself briefly blinded. No daughter of Mera and Taav would leap to her death this way, bewildered and fearful as a beast. Fiercely, Shadow drew upon the clarity, and through it saw the three Radiants who faced her. Two were men. The third was Hakin.

She had never before looked at her father's widow with the clarity, and doing so shocked her, for she saw not the surface loveliness but the reality. A ghastly being, filled with some unnatural essence, the skin cadaverous beneath its youthful illusion. *What bargain has Hakin made with the grayvers?*

The Radiant leader raised her hands, to work a cage of burning light. Perhaps with more time, more knowledge, Shadow might have stood against her, but not now. Forcing a last smile, to show that she chose her fate freely, she leaped from the opening into the deadly river below.

Chapter Two

Cold stabbed at Shadow: cold rushing wind, icy churning water. The river closed above her head and she could not find the surface. Hampered by her injured shoulder, Shadow struggled weakly, without effect, until her lungs ached with old air.

A small firm thing, like a button, pressed against her neck, and, mercifully, something tugged her across the current. If this was the Radiants' doing they were welcome to her.

The stony riverbank scraped her skin, and the cold renewed its assault, but Shadow felt only her lungs, gasping in the air as a starving man crams his belly with food, pain mingling with relief.

Sated at last, she lay shivering. Something snuffled at her with its button nose, dripping and casting a strange image beneath the triple moons which, tonight, were ranged across the sky. The ring-babble uttered an eager yip. It feinted at her playfully, sharp-muzzled head cocked, bushy tail corkscrewing with enthusiasm. The black rings around its furred body were barely perceptible in the moonlight.

This ringer was knee-high, larger than most, perhaps because it lived outside the city and caught more prey. The creatures were despised for their stupidity and their blind trust. You could kick them and starve them, but they always came back.

Still, this one had saved her life. Perhaps it even knew where to find shelter.

The Radiants? Shadow turned and scanned the river but saw no sign of pursuit. She would have liked to use the clarity, but did not dare drain herself further; besides, it didn't reach far. Most likely they would assume she had died. But it would be wise to remove herself in case they sent out a searching light.

And yet . . . Nle. Would he be given next month, or could he hold out longer, perhaps hiding behind others in the cell when the tribute was selected? In any case, she had no way of helping him now.

"Come on." Shadow led the capering ring-babble into the darkness.

She tried to remember what she could of the countryside around Ad-Omaq, but she had been a child when last she saw it, before the ghouls roamed the land. And tonight the trifurcated moonlight distorted her vision. Shadow vaguely recalled the surrounding flatlands as dimpled with farms, but in this dim glow each hillock and bush loomed at her, warped and threatening. Did something move, just beyond her line of sight?

She considered whether to aim for one of the few inhabited farmhouses. Here she might find a warm fire and ready food, but more likely a spear. Since ordinary men and women no longer dared walk abroad at night, anyone hearing her approach would read a threat in it. She must go warily, assuming as in the city that everyone was an enemy until proven otherwise.

Chills wracked her, fed equally by her eerie surroundings and the penetrating wetness of her robe. Shadow halted, hearing the ringer mutter worriedly at her side with half-human babbling sounds. She laid one hand on its neck and felt a warm, furry quickening in her veins, as if the creature had loaned her some of its strength. Closing her eyes, Shadow dared to draw on the clarity.

The land had changed greatly since she and Mera had passed through it. Many of the farmhouses were deserted and falling into ruin. Nevertheless, some farm animals remained, and kitchen gardens sprouted edible plants among the weeds. Ghouls walked the land, but there were none nearby.

Pinpointing an empty house not far away, Shadow released the clarity and waited for the inevitable rush of exhaustion. But although her mind blurred for a moment, she recovered more readily than usual. Perhaps the ring-babble, its hot little tongue licking affectionately at her wrist, truly had given her some of its fortitude.

Pain wrenched at Shadow's shoulder as they walked, and her knees were threatening to give way by the time they came to the house. Once in the yard, the ring-babble darted from her side, and she heard the squawk of a harkbird as it died.

Shadow pushed open the creaking door. Moonlight touched the inside only dimly, through chinks in the logs and one window from which the burlap covering had fallen away. There was but a single large room, a fireplace at its head and the utensils of everyday life—straw-stuffed mattress, iron pots, a broom, clay bowls—standing about as if waiting to be used.

Heaping up wood along with a handful of straw

kindling, Shadow lit a fire with a sparker stolen from a caravan years ago. Protected by the warmth, she stripped off her soaked clothing and wrapped herself in a blanket she found folded in one corner.

The ring-babble, with the simple-minded devotion of its kind, brought the bird to her instead of eating it on the spot. Shadow slit the prey with her knife and tossed the entrails to the animal, then spitted the bird and let it char while she laid out her bedding to dry in front of the fire.

The residents of this place must have left hurriedly, and not long ago, for the utensils bore only a thin layer of dust. Whatever had happened to the people, Shadow could spare them no more than a morsel of pity. In the streets she'd learned that he who wouldn't strike first was first to be struck.

Weariness and hunger tugged at her, but she must make the place secure. What it took to keep out the foul things of the night, she didn't know, for the evils of the countryside were of quite a different nature than those of Ad-Omaq. But ignorance was no excuse for carelessness.

The door was easily bolted, and the burlap replaced across the window to block the firelight. Meager protection, that, but ring-babbles slept lightly, and Shadow herself was in the habit of dozing with frequent awakenings, so they might have some warning.

Then there was the matter of the injured shoulder. Cursing the bloodcat, she dug into her pack for a vial of silver liquid. A drop of it, soothed over the crusting scab, eased away the pain.

Chores completed, Shadow tore the bird from its spit and ripped off bits with her teeth. The flesh was warm but mostly raw, a matter of little consequence.

Sated, she lay before the fire, letting its heat play across her face. Unexpectedly, her mind filled with memories of a home much like this, her mother's cottage in the hills.

Mera was of the ancient peoples, many of whom had degenerated through inbreeding into strange mutations. But she had inherited the untainted talents of the old race. She could look at a thing or a person and see its true nature and sometimes reach into its mind. How much of Mera was in Shadow's clarity, and how much of Taav?

Her thoughts drifting into vagueness, Shadow slept. She awoke later and listened carefully to the night sounds. Gabble of harkbirds, moan of a night wind, scurry of munts beneath the floorboards. Nothing more.

The fire renewed itself hungrily with the logs she heaped on. Shadow glanced at the ring-babble, which regarded her and muttered softly.

"Why are you here?" she asked it, feeling as if its chatter deserved a reply. "Why should you care what happens to me?"

For answer, it crawled closer and laid one tan paw on her knee. The black eyes looked wistful, but perhaps that was its natural expression. It was lonely. And so, she knew with a shock, was she. Restless these last two months, thinking it due to worry for her friends, she only now recognized the feeling.

Or perhaps it was being in this cottage, so much like the one she had grown up in, that brought back memories of childhood when visits from her bold father had enlivened their monotonous lives.

Taav, although a Radiant, chafed at the restrictions of the city. Despite the arrogance to which he had been bred, he held no grudge against the horned

people and believed an adept should travel through
the land to learn its true character.

Against the opposition of his wife, Hakin, he journeyed through Omaq to the mountains where a few
of the old race remained. In a remote valley, he had
met Mera, the wise woman, who lived a hard life
farming and hunting and telling fortunes for peasants.

Whether he loved Mera, Shadow never knew, but
he got her with child in the same year as his wife,
and so they were born, the girls Mera-ti and Briala.
Taav made no secret of having two daughters, and
two women; in the end, his loose tongue cost Mera
her life.

It was his grin Shadow remembered best, and the
childish delight he took in his ability to narrow a
beam of light and chop a tree neatly into logs. Then
he would build a leaping fire and sit beside it telling
stories of his travels, of how he had passed as a
trader and penetrated the forest of Kir, of how he
watched colored lights dance through the sky as the
new Mage, silver-haired despite his youth, took his
place as ruler.

And there were tales of the many-masted ships
that arrived in Ad-Kir from Ad-Son and other cities
across the ocean, for Kir had the only port in the
Eastern Lands. Although Omaq too touched the ocean,
its coast was rocky and harsh, and only the brave or
the foolhardy dared weigh anchor and put to shore in
small boats. Now that ghouls stalked the land, of
course, even the fiercest of adventurers no longer
attempted it, and when the Mage closed the forest to
trade a half dozen years ago, Ad-Omaq had been left
isolated. But Taav had not lived to see that.

When Shadow was five, her father became leader
of the Radiants, and after that he visited only twice.

How long the days had dragged, for her and her mother. For weeks after each visit, the little girl would run to the door half a dozen times a day, thinking she heard harthorn hoofs on the path, or a man chuckling over some new escapade. Each time the pain came afresh, that Taav was not here, that he had another life and another daughter to hold in his arms.

He died when Shadow was eight, not long after one of his visits. When word came of the great ceremonial funeral to be held, Mera would not rest until she and her child journeyed to Ad-Omaq. Hakin must have been watching, and identified her by the small girl who looked nearly a twin to Briala. Mera was seized, and her horns revealed, and she was slain for daring to enter the city. Mera's death came shortly before the grayvers emerged and claimed their monthly tribute, or she might have been given to them instead.

As the crowd thronged around Mera at her capture, shouting and jeering, Shadow felt herself thrust away. It was her mother's attempt to save her, she knew now, but then she felt only a numbing terror at the towering bodies that shoved and shouted around her. In her confusion, she careened straight into a boy and knocked him flat. A coin-purse flew from his hand and was snatched by a woman in the crowd.

"Curse you!" snarled the boy, jumping to his feet.

At that moment a merchant standing nearby yelled that his coin-purse had been stolen. Enforcers found it in the woman's possession and dragged her off.

The boy grinned. "That's luck for you."

"I saved you!" Shadow piped up, desperate to cling to someone.

"Luck. That's all." The boy darted away without a backward glance. Shadow chased after him.

For a day and a half she followed Nle through the city, not knowing what else to do. It amazed her that he could survive this way, without adults, living off what he stole or begged. She knew the Enforcers might be looking for her, yet Shadow maintained her pursuit doggedly until exhaustion and hunger overcame her and she sank down on a doorstep, crying.

A few minutes later, Nle stopped in front of her. "Well?" he said. "You giving up?" She just sobbed. He looked uncomfortable. Then, grudgingly, he stuck a piece of bread into her hand.

After that, he allowed her to accompany him, finding her a scarf to hide her horns and teaching her the tricks of thieving and hiding. She grew to think of him as her brother. Through him, Shadow learned the secrets of Ad-Omaq—the Den of Ashi, the Street of Lost Women, the underground gardens where slaves toiled, the indolent Highborns who satisfied their perverted tastes with slave youngsters.

It was two years later that a pair of Enforcers came upon the children as they slept in an alley and seized them. Nle bit one of their captors, who kicked him brutally.

A sudden footstep, and someone huge stepped out behind them, grasped the Enforcers and smashed their heads together. Shadow gaped up at a pale giant whose silver eyes gave him an air of depravity.

"Run, you little fool!" snapped Nle, hobbling away on his shattered leg. Shadow dashed after him.

"No, please. Wait." To their alarm the giant followed. Shadow slipped through a crack in a wall but Nle's leg slowed him and the man caught his arm. "I won't hurt you. My name is Dorf. I want to be your friend."

A peasant. Shadow was reminded of her own arrival as Dorf told of coming with his family after ghouls slew his father. But in Ad-Omaq, Enforcers had enslaved his mother and sister while he sought food. Today he had avenged them by saving the children.

Nle wanted nothing to do with the half-witted giant, but when he tried to scurry away his leg gave out and he collapsed. Dorf carried him to a safer place far from the slain Enforcers and kept watch for the next days. Even when Nle recovered, it was clear he would never be the same. They needed Dorf's strength to survive. So their makeshift union was formed, and it endured until Nle's and Dorf's arrest.

Her thoughts returning to the present, Shadow poked idly at a box that sat beside the fire. The lid clattered off, startling a yip from the ring-babble and revealing a welcome cache of dried fruits. Chewing on a handful of them, Shadow lay back on her pile of blankets. She could not imagine Nle turned into a ghoul, his quick mind blotted out. Vowing anew to rescue him, she dozed until morning.

Shadow awoke to a chill room and a yellow glaze filtering through the masked windows. The ring-babble chattered impatiently at the door, and she let it out. The farmyard looked forsaken, the fowl cages empty and a metal plow lying exposed. Beyond stretched the fields, separated by windbreaks of bent trees.

Shadow flexed her shoulder. It remained slightly stiff, but any danger of infection had been removed by the medicine—stolen half a dozen years ago from the last caravan to come through the forest. Using the shoulder gingerly, she searched through the paraphernalia of the house for foodstuffs as she considered her next step.

She might remain here for a while, but the city loomed much too close. And she could not bear to sit idle as Nle's days dwindled.

It was pointless to head south, where the sea would block her. And in the mountains of the north lurked the grayvers.

To the west lay the barren lands. Here roved fierce bands of outcasts and renegades. Perhaps, like Argen, they wanted women; she might survive there, a chattel like the decaying flesh on the Street of Lost Women. But that was worse than no life at all, and it could not help Nle.

That left only the east, and the forest of Kir. Closed, now. But what did that mean? Even before the last few years, the forest had been open only to traders for half a century. From what Taav had said, there were neither Enforcers nor weapons to keep intruders out. The Mage of Kir had no need of them.

Taav had said the traders were forbidden to leave the path, but he, disguised as one of them, had stepped from it several times, to test the Mage's powers. He told of a bloodcat that leaped at him from nowhere, and fell to earth when he retreated as though it had struck an invisible wall. In another place, he said, the earth beneath him sheered off suddenly, leaving an abyss that he barely escaped by jumping backward. And, he said, the merchants had thrown away their maps, for the path changed each time they traveled it, although it began and ended as before.

"No land can exist in such a state of flux," Mera had protested. "Bloodcats that come from nowhere, paths that will not be charted, abysses that open up as you stand there—there must be some pattern to it all." But if there was, no one had found it.

And now the forest was closed entirely. Yet might it not be possible, with the clarity, to find some way in?

On the other side lay the city of Ad-Kir. The Mage was the enemy of Ad-Omaq; well, perhaps not openly, for he had not attacked it, but certainly he held no friendship for the Radiants. And there was more in Ad-Kir than the Mage: mercenary ships, and travelers from Ad-Son and Kirrillea and Sajawak, from cities and lands whose names Taav had recited like poetry. If the Mage would not help her, there still might be others in Ad-Kir who could be hired or persuaded to rescue Nle. Shadow would trade what she could or steal what she must; the port-city was rich, and the thieving easy, or so the storytellers claimed in the sneakways of Ad-Omaq.

Or perhaps she would have the luck to find some band of well-armed adventurers who could be lured with a greater prize. Shadow knew the ways of the underworld of Ad-Omaq and, from her spying, had learned that there was dissension even among the Radiants themselves, for not all were as self-serving as Hakin and Briala. Perhaps a plan might be devised to overthrow the Radiants by stealth and claim the city. Who had a better right than Shadow? And whatever booty the adventurers demanded in return for their help, it could be no more than the Radiants already plundered from their own peasantry.

True, Shadow had formed no plan for such an overthrow, and her clarity was of little use against the Radiants' light-weapons. But there were other powers from other lands, as yet unknown in Omaq, so Taav had said. And where better to find them than in Ad-Kir?

And so, determined to go east, Shadow concluded her search of the cabin. It had been more fruitful than she expected. There were nuts and dried meats, evidence that the inhabitants hadn't had time to pack for their departure, and a black hooded cape made of thick wool, to replace the tattered garment that had served her far too long. Best of all were the boots, heavy ones made of tanned hide. Stuffed with shredded cloth, they fit well enough.

She also took the best of the blankets. Autumn lay upon the land, with its morning frosts and cold nights that turned one's breath to ice. In the city one might sleep wedged against the brick house of a Highborn family, absorbing some of the heat that radiated outward. There was none of that here.

Shadow tucked her goods into a pack and hoisted it. Despite the weight, she dared not load any of it on the ring-babble. There was no telling when the beast might dart away and vanish. Besides, she knew the burden would lighten soon enough as the food disappeared.

The ringer joined Shadow outside the house, capering as if delighted by the expedition. The sun was almost overhead, a reminder to hurry. Shadow spared one last look at the spires of Ad-Omaq. From here the sloping city looked smaller than its actual size; it was as much vertical as horizontal, life beehiving within the semisoft rock. Distance lessened its terrors, as well. How fearful the Den of Ashi loomed in the city, and how insignificant the thought of it struck her now.

She swung away across the flat lands, marking her course by the sun. At least there was no fear of losing her path, even at night, for in time of need there was always the clarity. It was proving more useful in this new life of hers than it had been in the old.

Striding along, Shadow kept alert for signs of life. The ground was hard and yielded no clear prints of any kind. Here and there she spotted a harthorn leaping across a field. The usually placid creatures had gone wild, and gave her plenty of berth. Too bad; she remembered well enough from childhood how to milk one, and ride one, and butcher it when it ceased to serve her well.

As the hours lengthened, Shadow thought perhaps the ring-babble would turn back, for it had no doubt established a nest somewhere. But it stayed beside her, nosing away now and then to fetch a munt or other small creature.

Only once did Shadow see another human being, a man in rough peasant's garb who passed some distance away, his feet dragging the ground as he rode upon a dwarf harthorn. He glared at her and lifted a shovel menacingly. She shot him a city gesture of disrespect and continued on her way.

Nothing else threatened, and that was enough to raise Shadow's spirits. Her mind wove fantasies of returning with the Mage, of watching as he shattered the walls of the Citadel and Hakin came crawling out. But it troubled her to think of Omaq being taken by Kir. The Kirites might be kinder than the Radiants, but they would be conquerors. Better a band of ruffians who could be bought off or overpowered if they proved ambitious.

Shadow ate on the march, for the daylight hours were too precious to waste. By twilight, the unaccustomed boots chafed, and she was grateful when a crumbling farmhouse came into sight a few fields off.

However, her good cheer vanished when she and the ring-babble arrived at the yard. Heaped beside the cottage and just beginning to bloat with lyworms lay the brown body of a harthorn lamb, its throat torn out.

Ghouls. They drank the blood of living things. The body was fresh, too fresh even to stink. It must have been killed the night before.

The ring-babble murmured worriedly. There were no other animals in the yard, not a harkbird nor a living harthorn nor even, so far as one could see, a munt. Shadow stared about nervously. Ghouls didn't walk in the light, from what she'd heard, but dark was falling rapidly, and they might lurk nearby. Perhaps even in this farmhouse. Wearily, she summoned the clarity.

The house was dilapidated, with tiles missing from the roof, and the interior had been stripped, although by whom there was no telling. It contained only a broken table, a churn, and a few other heavy pieces of furniture. Nothing stirred there.

Already the last rays of the sun were fading. Shadow circled to the well and pulled up the bucket, scraping aside the film of algae on top. She and the ring-babble drank deeply. The creature pressed close to her legs as she headed indoors. They would eat no fresh meat tonight.

Shadow sealed herself and the ring-babble inside as best she could. Then, with much effort, she broke apart the legs of the table and heaped them on the fireplace, but without kindling the sparks sang briefly against the blackness and died. Shadow searched in her pack and drew out her old robe.

It should burn readily, and it was, after all, a tattered, stained thing. Nle had stolen it years ago from a line of washing in the courtyard of a rich merchant. What a game Shadow had made of trying it on in the alley where they'd retreated, walking with the mincing steps of a Highborn girl and posing as if to display a necklace of gemstones. Her friends cheered her on, laughing. Now, huddled before the chill hearth of an abandoned farmhouse, she tore the thing into strips and set the sparker to it. A flare of heat enveloped the wood.

Shadow sank back beside the ring-babble and tugged off her boots. Surely one should waste no sorrow on a bit of ruined cloth. It was Nle she wanted back. And Dorf, but he was gone. Oh, but she had debts to square with the Radiants, however long it took. "Guard your walls well, Hakin," she murmured.

"Guard your walls well."

Shadow whipped about, jerking the knife from her belt and crouching to face whoever or whatever had echoed her words. The toneless, low voice had sifted through a crack in the roof. While she was absorbed in her fire making, someone must have climbed there. Now she heard the scrape of tiles being pulled aside, in not one but three or perhaps four places.

The first shape dropped into view, a man's form, the eyes glittering white in the firelight. The ghouls had found her.

Chapter Three

Three dark-robed ghouls crouched facing Shadow, their eyes blank in the firelight, and she could hear a fourth scrabbling on the roof. They were former tradesmen or farmers, no doubt, perhaps with families. She might have been moved to pity if there had been any humanity left in them, but these were only bodies with lightless eyes and a hunger for blood. Sweat filmed her palms, and she shifted the knife uneasily.

In Ad-Omaq, under Nle's tutelage, each danger had been defined and prepared for. But here, alone in this cabin, there was only the unknown.

"What do you want?" Shadow noted with scorn that her voice trembled. City-hardened, she tolerated no weakness in herself.

"What do you want?" mocked the ghouls. It seemed they could only repeat her words, twisting them to taunt her.

They carried no weapons, but there were three of them. And their slavering mouths gaped to reveal fangs as the things surrounded her slowly, seeming to take pleasure in prolonging the terror.

The ring-babble thrust its cold nose into Shadow's

palm and mumbled worriedly. She could no more save it than she could save herself, or Nle. But she would teach those cursed ghouls a thing or two about city fighting before they took her.

Without warning, the ring-babble leaped forward, teeth bared. One of the ghouls hurled it impatiently against the wall, where it slid to the ground and lay limp.

Shadow reached behind her into the fire and pulled out a flaming table leg. She whipped the brand so sparks danced across the room, and for the first time the ghouls halted their advance.

"What do you want?" rasped one of the ghouls with an obscene smile, again echoing her last words, and the others laughed, a hollow sound like the slither of a serpent. At that moment, a fourth shape plunged through one of the roof openings, not stealthy as its mates were but landing heavily. Even at this angle, Shadow could see it was larger than the others.

The distraction gave her an opening. She lunged, knife in one hand, torch in the other. A blink of white, shocked eyes, and then one ghoul beat the air, his garment flaming, while a companion shuddered backward, blood pouring from his gut.

The third snarled, edging around her with a gesture to the larger ghoul. In her attack, Shadow had left the protection of the fire, and now she had an enemy on each side. Best to destroy the thing behind her before the huge latecomer moved into action.

Shadow whirled, barely in time. The ghoul leaped at her, hands reaching for her shoulders and teeth positioned to rip out her throat. The sheer weight of him bore her to the ground. Her wrist struck the dirt floor and the torch fell from her grasp. The knife remained, but the fiend had her pinned. Its white eyes bored into hers, pulling, pulling, as though to suck out her insides. It was taking her soul. For the grayvers. But this was only a ghoul, a thing once-human. She pitted her strength against it, locking them motionless. . . .

Then something crashed into her attacker, knocking him off balance and into a tangled mass. For a disoriented moment, she thought it was the ring-babble.

No. The fourth ghoul, confused by the uproar, had attacked one of its fellows.

Shadow dragged herself up. The old bloodcat wound in her right shoulder bled freely and the pain seared. She must get away before the creature discovered its error.

But her pack lay beyond the writhing bodies, by the fire. Without food, medicine, boots, she could not survive.

Shadow crept toward the hearth. The two ghouls thrashing on the floor paid no heed as she gathered the pack. Now she had the boots as well, but the ring-babble lay just beyond. Curse it, an animal meant nothing, yet she hesitated, and as she did, the smaller ghoul moaned and lay still.

Its slayer lumbered to his feet. Shadow froze. There was still the knife, but . . .

. . . but the hulking creature facing her was Dorf.

A welt reddened on his cheek, below the eyes that had the blank unnatural gleam of a ghoul. Or was that only an illusion wrought by firelight on their always-pale surfaces? How could he be Dorf, and not be Dorf? How could she kill him, and yet how could she let him kill her?

"Shadow," he said.

It took a moment for the significance to sink in. He recognized her. He could frame his own words.

"Dorf!" She flew into his arms, embracing the giant, kind-hearted brute, starting to cry. And he, wondering, said over and over again, "Shadow. What are you doing here?"

Finally she stepped away and looked at him. "I thought you were a ghoul."

"So did they."

She glanced about, at the three bodies, one charred, one stained with darkening blood, one twisted at the neck. "Let's clear them out."

Together, they hauled the things into the farmyard. Shadow would have preferred to bury them; after all, they had been men once. But she had no tool to dig with, and no energy to spare for grave making.

They returned to the house. Shadow pulled Dorf down beside her on a blanket before the fire and cradled the ring-babble as it began to wake. "Tell me what happened, Dorf. And Nle, how was he when you left him?"

"Restless," said the big fellow. The single word conjured an image of the dagger-thin young man, limping about a dank prison cell, probing every crevice, listening for guards' footsteps, turning every remote possibility for escape over and over like a munt examining a piece of fruit.

"I tried to rescue him and nearly got caught myself." Shadow hugged her knees. "Tell me what happened to you."

In halting words, he told of being marched from the city and taken by the Enforcers to the mountains. He quivered as he spoke, and Shadow slipped one arm around his shoulders. Despite his bulk, one always wanted to protect Dorf. "The grayvers—what were they like?"

"Empty."

"Empty?"

He struggled to explain, forming a shape in the air with his hands. "They wear gray robes."

She knew he was doing his best, but that couldn't entirely stem her impatience. There was disagreement in the city as to whether the Gray Ones had shape and substance, or were mere puffs of smoke that could change form or even vanish entirely. "And beneath the robes?"

He shook his head.

This was getting them nowhere. "What color are their eyes?"

"They don't have eyes."

He was anxious, wanting to please but unable to find the words. The tension was making things worse, Shadow knew, and besides, she could no longer ignore the throb in her shoulder. Reaching into the pack, she drew out the ointment and pulled down her robe to bare the wound. Dorf took the medicine and rubbed in a drop of it, so gently he might have been stroking a child. Shadow smiled with relief. "It's good to have you back."

"Good for me, too."

After a brief rest, she continued her questioning, gradually drawing out bits of information. The ghouls traveled in small packs, she learned. There seemed to be no organization to their rampages. The grayvers released them with only one command: that the creatures take souls before indulging their passion for blood. Not being able to do it himself, Dorf could tell her no more than that. But clearly, by some means, the souls were transferred to the grayvers, thus further strengthening them.

"How did you keep from becoming a ghoul?"

"When the grayvers came, when they . . . pulled at me, I—I tried to think of what Nle would do." Dorf drew closer to the fire. "He always said, If you can't win in a fair fight—"

"Cheat," Shadow finished for him, her voice softening at the thought of Nle.

"So I made my head empty. It wasn't hard. I guess I fooled them. But they took a little of—of whatever it is they take. I felt cold after that, for days and days. I still do."

Alone, Dorf had wandered back toward the city, avoiding the ghouls as best he could. Then, tonight, he'd come upon these three as they attacked the house. Hoping to rescue their intended victim, he had followed them inside.

"And saved my life. Now we must find a way to help Nle." Shadow's hand stroked absently across the ring-babble's fur.

Dorf's eyelids were drooping. He could labor for hours without pause, but talking always wearied him. Shadow covered him with the spare blanket. That her friend had escaped becoming a ghoul raised her hopes for Nle. The grayvers clearly were not so all-powerful as the city rumors claimed.

Shadow curled up beside her friend, pulling her blanket tight. She meant to think further about this new development, to reconsider her plans in the light of it, but in the double warmth she dozed and finally slept more soundly than she had in months.

In the morning, the rejuvenated ring-babble popped through the roof with a mouthful of nightcreeper. Dorf twisted the head off the lizard and used Shadow's knife to slit it for cooking.

She asked him more as the fragrance of roasting

nightcreeper filled the cottage, of the grayvers and whether they had a leader.

He poked at the lizard with a stick. "The Graylord. I saw him—for a minute. He's—cold. He felt evil. He's a grayver, I think, only so much bigger and—and distorted somehow."

Shadow could draw no further description from him. Finally she accepted a chunk of roasted lizard meat, as sweet as one of the Highborn's fowl. Dorf ate placidly beside her, lizard juice dripping down his chin.

From him, Shadow was able to learn that a dozen Enforcers accompanied the prisoners to the mountains —too many for a direct attack. But once the victims were released to the grayvers, there was no more need for guards.

"The grayvers . . . give commands. In your mind. You have to do what they say." Dorf's head began to sink, a sign of exhaustion.

"There must be a way." Shadow paced through the room, opening the door and staring north, to the mountains, thinking over what Dorf had told her.

Surely the Enforcers withdrew before actual contact with the grayvers. Surely in that moment it might be possible to reach Nle, to tell him of the trick Dorf had found, so that he too could escape.

There would be time enough then to think of fleeing to Kir, when the three of them were together.

Shadow turned back into the room. "Come on." She jostled Dorf awake. "It's a long way to the mountains."

Chapter Four

By the next night, the towers of Ad-Omaq had dwindled behind them into a child's toy, while ahead the mountains had scarcely grown. Only by measuring them mentally against the height of the trees could Shadow be sure they were nearer.

She and Dorf followed the course of the Omaq River. They saw no farmhouse nearby at dusk, and made camp in a small grove by a stream, where a bit of cloth from Shadow's pack served as a net.

"This smells good." Dorf roasted their catch on a spit over the fire.

Shadow, her hunger stronger than the searing pain of her fingers, began peeling the burned scales from a fish. "After we get Nle, we'll go east."

"But Kir is closed."

"So they say. But maybe . . ."

"Shadow." Dorf cut her off. "Something's coming."

He possessed unusually keen hearing, Shadow knew. Even straining, she could make out no sounds in the thick darkness beyond the small circle of firelight.

"Ghouls?" she whispered.

"No. Not footsteps."

Grayvers had never been observed this far south. Once, Mera had said, there were other beasts in these parts, but they had been driven out long ago by the farmers. Pressing Dorf's shoulder for reassurance, Shadow closed her eyes and sought the clarity. It came in a surge.

A great viscous mass swished toward them, writhing with lywormlike tentacles. Body and head in a slimy heap, eight eyes bulging from stalks, it billowed out a dozen tentacles, searching the darkness for prey. Victims would be stuffed whole into its swollen belly, kept alive as bit by bit their limbs began to putrefy and were digested.

"An ormgrim." Shadow felt Dorf grow rigid. In his days as a farmer he, too, must have heard of the foul things.

The beast slithered closer. One could hear it gabbling, almost feel its damp heat. Could it be tricked, distracted somehow? Shadow needed to see past the horror, into the thing's gut.

The clarity—never before had it been pushed so hard, strained to reach beyond itself. And then, a leaping out, or in; through the ormgrim's eyes, she saw herself and Dorf and the ring-babble outlined by flickering red, and hunger raged through her, flesh-hunger.

A high-pitched cry restored her to herself as the ring-babble darted forward through the night, across the clearing toward the predator. There was a leap, a scream of agony, and then the slurping of lyworm-tentacles filled the air.

After a while, the eating sounds died away and the ormgrim, sated, moved off. Mera had said the things ate only once in three or four days. Shadow hoped the ring-babble would die quickly in the monster's innards.

She watched the rest of the fish char on the fire, still alert for the ormgrim. From time to time her hand cupped instinctively as if awaiting the thrust of a small cold nose.

It was only as she lay falling asleep, with Dorf keeping watch for the first half of the night, that it occurred to her why the clarity had come so strongly. It was Dorf, his power. She could draw energy from others. Another thing she hadn't known in the city.

Nor had she known that she could reach into another's mind and see through alien eyes. This could be a dangerous gift, Shadow reflected. Once a channel was opened, who knew what might come of it?

And there remained the possibility her gift would strengthen as they neared the mountains, as Mera had foretold. It must tap ancient sources. As did the grayvers, perhaps. From what little she knew of them, Shadow surmised that they, too, could reach into others' minds, to take the warm essence of a human. Her gift must be related to theirs, but not, she hoped, too closely.

Shadow's musings drifted back over the past few days, over all she had learned and seen. Hakin was linked somehow to the grayvers, she felt certain of it. And whatever Hakin had taken from them, Briala valued it even more than her mother did.

Other images flitted through Shadow's tired thoughts —the Enforcer collapsing before her knife thrust, the slimy trek through the sewers, the stink of the Den of Ashi. And Argen. Would he really have helped her escape if he could? More likely he wanted only what other men desired, those things that meant so little to Shadow: her face, the shape of her body. She slept then, and dreamed, not of Argen but of some other, whose gaze swept across her like sunlight.

She stood watch the second half of the night, without incident. Neither she nor Dorf slept enough, yet she dared not waste any more time on resting until Nle was safe.

In the next days, as the mountains grew, the landscape began to alter. Fissures appeared in the earth, hinting at the caves that pocked the landscape further north. Shadow had poked into one in her childhood, and been snatched away by Mera with a sharp warning about ancient evils. But it was only after Mera's death that the grayvers became powerful; after Taav's death, too.

On Taav's last visit, Shadow remembered her mother pleading with him. He had planned to delve into the caves. The leader of the Radiants must know everything about his land, he said. And he *had* survived, had returned to Ad-Omaq afterward, only to die a few weeks later. But of what, Shadow had never known. And what unnatural spirit was it that pulsed within Hakin's flesh, revealing itself only beneath the clarity? If there was a sense to these fragments that taunted Shadow on the weary march north, she could not find it.

Food was scarce, and they had to dig into the ever-shrinking pack. With Dorf's aid, Shadow dared use the clarity more, picking out a huddle of stones for a night's shelter or a burrow of munts to harvest for dinner, but it was scarcely enough. The breeze carried a chill autumn tang. Winter might soon catch them helpless as peasants in the city.

Late one afternoon, in the foothills of the mountains, they observed a tumbledown shack. Shadow thought of the two farmhouses that had given her shelter: one a refuge, one a trap. You took your chances.

Crossing toward it, they halted at the sight of a harthorn lamb tethered in the open grass. It bleated sadly, a cry answered from behind the structure, where its mother must be secured. Who would have tied it there? Not ghouls. Still, Shadow had no desire to meet whoever lived in the shelter.

Yet as she signaled Dorf to give the place wide berth, a man came out, a solidly built fellow with a full beard. He noticed them at once and called his companions. There were six in all, three rough-looking men, two women and a slender boy of seven or eight.

Dorf looked at Shadow. "Bandits?"

"Their packs are too heavy." She gestured at a heap near the door of the dwelling. Robbers would travel light. Nor were they farmers; these fields had not been plowed in many a year. What was it she sensed in them? Curiosity, but little fear. Not like the panic-stricken peasants crowding into Ad-Omaq.

The pale late-autumn sunlight was fading. They needed to find shelter soon. And these were people, after all, the first she and Dorf had seen. "We might as well take the risk," she said. "Now that they've spotted us."

One of the men, smaller than the others but with an air of alert confidence, was walking toward them. He held an ax, not in a threatening way but ready to use if it proved necessary. "Show us your weapons."

Shadow held up her knife.

"And him?"

"He has only his hands." She reached over and shook Dorf's robe, so they could hear there was no clink of metal.

"You travel unarmed?" It was one of the women, disbelieving, trailing after the man. "Where are your beasts? And your eyes are strange, both of you."

To give them a lie? No invention could accommodate all these oddities. "We come from the city," Shadow began.

"No one comes from the city," said the small man.

"We do," said Shadow.

"Look." The second woman joined them. "She has horns."

"You're fugitives, then." The man leaned on his ax, studying Shadow. "You have the eyes of a Radiant. And horns. Yes, we will give you shelter; you are an outcast like us." He ignored a muttered remark from one of the women. "I am Migal."

Shadow introduced herself and Dorf. Grudgingly, Migal's companions stood aside to let them enter the shack. Only the boy betrayed an eager curiosity, following close at their heels.

Inside, a small fire vented poorly through a hole in the roof, filling the place with smoke. But it was warm, and the walls provided a measure of safety. By the fire lay some bones, gnawed clean. Harthorns? They were too large to be anything else, yet the people did not look ill-fed, and it seemed odd that they would eat their few pack animals.

Shadow thought of the lamb, tethered out in the field. A lure? There must be animals living in these parts that were unknown to her. More than ever, she was glad of the night's shelter.

Dinner was a shared meal, dried fruit from Shadow's pack, vegetables and fish from the small stores of their hosts. She sketched their tale quickly, saying no more than she must. In turn, Migal told her that his band had been farmers, but now lived as best they could.

"You are wise not to go to the city," Shadow said.

One of the women spat on the floor. "We're not fools. The Radiants abused us even when our farms yielded well."

"We rely on no one but ourselves," said Migal. "We know the city won't protect us."

"It's left to us to handle the ghouls," the woman snarled.

"Ghouls killed her children," the other woman whispered to Shadow.

"And now, will you share a drink with us?" said Migal.

They drank wine from a jug, a bittersweet liquor of the kind that could dull the mind, so Shadow took only a little. None of the group drank much. Migal was watching her; he was the one man who lacked a woman. She knew that look by now.

This might be a trap. Her meager pack could be the lure, or she herself. But Shadow felt no evil here, only anger, and it was not directed at her or Dorf.

The young boy was posted as guard. Shadow, exhausted by lack of rest, was grateful for the chance to sleep the night through. Again, she saw Migal watching as she curled up next to Dorf. She meant to keep an eye open until he fell asleep, but weariness brought slumber quickly.

A scream woke her. For a dazed moment, she thought someone had attacked the guard-boy. Then she realized it was his voice calling out, "Hurry! They've come!" The men and women scurried and groped about the shack, racing out with knives and axes. Dorf sat up beside her. "What's going on?"

Shadow joined him in the doorway. The horizon was gray with pre-dawn, and she made out a struggling mass in the field and heard hoarse shouts and curses. Drawing power from her friend, she saw truly. Blood and slaughter, but not of animals. . . .

"Ghouls." The word stuck in her throat. "They've lured them and now they're killing them." Her mind flicked back to the bones lying beside the fire.

"They . . . they eat ghouls?" Dorf stood in a daze of disbelief, until Shadow pulled him into the shelter to gather their belongings.

Out in the field, the yelling died away and chopping sounds drifted toward the shack. Like so many wild beasts, the ghouls were being hacked to pieces.

An unreasoning panic drove Shadow to be away before their hosts returned. She had killed men in the city, and once a woman, a wiry girl who tried to choke Shadow and steal her pack. She had killed ghouls, too, that night in the farmhouse. But always in the heat of struggle, not with this cold butchery. Even the wretched patrons of Ashi shunned human flesh.

The pack was assembled, tied across Dorf's broad back. Shadow led the way out, grateful that their hosts had not returned. And then she saw the boy, standing there watching them.

"It's nearly dawn," Shadow said. "We have to be going."

"But there's a good kill!" They had taken only a few steps before he added, "It's all right, you know. They owe it to us."

Shadow broke into a lope, not stopping until she and Dorf were out of sight beyond some trees. Then words poured out of her. "Curse the grayvers. And curse Hakin. She's brought us to this."

"Shadow," Dorf said. "The Radiants never helped anyone but themselves."

"Taav would have fought the grayvers!"

"Not for us," said Dorf. "None of them ever cared about us, Shadow."

Taav. His handsome face, and those bright yellow eyes, always restless. Taav who blew into their cabin like a fresh breeze, who made Mera laugh. And yet, how Mera had sobbed each time he left, and he never stayed to hold her. He had loved her like a plaything, a ring-babble.

Shadow felt as if, before her eyes, Taav was shrinking from a giant to an ordinary man, or something less.

He had spoken sometimes of his duty to his people. Was that only empty words? Under his rule, as before he was chosen, peasants had toiled to feed the Citadel, and half-starved urchins had been forced to serve the perverted whims of Highborns. His people.

Shadow had no more time to waste on her father's memory. "Let's go on," she said abruptly.

Chapter Five

They followed the river on through the foothills, keeping to cover. Here the ghouls marched even in daylight; several times bands passed not far off. Once Shadow spied robed figures that might be grayvers, but dared not use the clarity. It might accidentally penetrate too deeply, throw her mind into theirs as with the ormgrim, and alert them to her presence.

Food was scarce in the autumn of Omaq. Even the hela-nuts were withered and few. The foothills had changed since the days of Shadow's childhood, become sparse and threatening, and always gloomy. Where she remembered flowers, stunted shrubs clung to rocks. Where the mornings had been clear, now fog pooled in the hollows, creeping upward at night and lingering. In the grayness, trees loomed blackly.

They made camp near where Dorf said the grayvers had met the tribute-prisoners, and waited for several days, huddling below a rocky outcropping that cut the wind. Between Shadow and Dorf grew a closeness that had not been there before. First had been Nle, then the three of them; never before had she and Dorf been alone together.

They did not share many words, although sometimes Shadow talked as if to herself. She had the cold hours to think back to her childhood, of the mountain peasants who had feared Mera, revering her when she helped to cure a child and despising her when she kept apart from their rough celebrations. Shadow had spent much time alone, dreaming of the crystal-white Citadel and weaving fantasies of someday meeting her sister.

Briala. To the lonely young Mera-ti, the name sparkled. They would be friends, share secrets, laugh together and need no one else. Later, in the city, had come the bitterness, that Briala should wear velvet and gemstones while Shadow lived in rags, hunted like an animal. Proud of her city slyness, Shadow came to disdain her sister, who faced no test to survive. Yet always she felt the uneasy link between them, a bond that could be broken only by death.

So the days passed. Finally, one frosty morning as she and Dorf finished their meager breakfast, they heard a man shout far off. Shadow had known the tribute-victims might be near, yet in this wasteland the human sound startled her. The river ran just out of sight to their left, and the yell had come from that direction. She pressed her hands to her temples, concentrating, searching for Nle.

There were six or seven Enforcers and perhaps a dozen chained men. The clarity did not find Nle among them. She and Dorf could watch the tribute-taking this time, and learn, but it meant they must wait another month into the winter.

She recognized one of the men: Ashi. The innkeeper was paying dearly for the serpent that killed the bloodcat. Shadow was sorry, a little. Ashi had given her finot, when he might have been rid of her.

Another shout rang from the mountains, this one not of summoning but of fear, and the Enforcers fled. Gray shapes moved along the earth. Although the robes defined manlike forms, where the faces should have been was only a kind of mist. A chill diffused through her, a sense of ancient rot creeping out of the dark places.

Under silent command, the band from the city marched along the river path, ever northward, staggering as the way grew rocky and steep. The grayvers wafted alongside them, indifferent to the course and the men. One of the prisoners fell and could not rise. Two others hoisted the limp form across their own shoulders and the miserable band moved on.

Shadow and Dorf kept hidden, skirting boulders and brush, pushing hard to keep pace. They dared not light a fire that night, but took turns sleeping under a pile of blankets while the other guarded. Dinner was hardened pieces of fruit, a few nuts, and the last bit of salted harthorn meat.

At first light, they resumed following. The previous day's journey had been uphill, but now the land angled less steeply. Dorf had described a flat ledge, a tableland where the souls had been taken, and it might be near. The grayvers could have robbed their victims at the river, but here they would be closer to the caves. Perhaps that fact held a clue to some weakness, some way to save Nle.

By late afternoon, scrub brush gave way to trees with drooping leaf-heavy branches that rustled at the least breath. Carefully, fearful of detection, Dorf and Shadow penetrated upward until the woods ended at the rim of a plateau.

The band of men halted above them, shivering in the twilight. One lurched forward, struggling uselessly against the command in his mind. A grayver faced him and the man went rigid. In the silence between them, the earth darkened slowly. When at last the prisoner turned, the fear, the anger, the humanness were gone, and in the moonlight his eyes showed white.

The Graylord had not come. Nor, it seemed, was he needed. The grayvers stripped their victims methodically.

At last only two prisoners remained, one of them the injured man huddled on the ground. The other was Ashi. He faced his tormentor with scorn, and spoke, his voice oddly high-pitched. "I curse you." Hot spittle hissed against the gray robe, but already the mist creature was staring into his one eye. Ashi writhed, cursed, cried out, but in the end he yielded.

And in the yielding, as ever, he led. Before the grayvers could take the injured prisoner, the ghoul Ashi leaped snarling at the fallen man, straddled him, and tore the unresisting throat. Blood steamed across Ashi, and the other ghouls champed and clawed each other to taste it.

If the wind turned, they would smell Shadow's blood, and Dorf's. She pressed to the ground, feeling twigs dig into her flesh, inhaling the leaf mold, until the snarling sounds ended and the bloody things that had been men moved away through the night.

Still, Shadow would not use the clarity while the grayvers might linger. An hour passed, perhaps more, as her muscles stiffened. At last, whispering to Dorf to stay hidden, Shadow crept forward onto the plateau. Nothing moved. She arose and advanced, step by painful step, not trusting the silence. As Nle had said, *Even a trap doesn't move until it's sprung.*

And then—a sudden thrashing behind her, and a

shout. "Run, Shadow!" A crash followed, and then another. Loud enough to mask her footsteps as she ran back.

Below, Dorf stood braced against a tree, lashing about him with a thick branch as three ghouls circled. One lunged, but its teeth had not yet grown into fangs, and Dorf flung it away through the trees. It smashed into a trunk and slithered to the earth.

The other two ranged barely beyond the arc of the heavy branch. Sooner or later one would find an opening. Shadow edged toward them, knife poised. Dorf looked up and, following his gaze, so did the shorter of the ghouls.

Ashi. But this Ashi had ice for eyes, and a snarling mouth ready to rip the pulse from her throat. Even as his companion dived forward to lock hand to hand with Dorf, Ashi stalked his newfound prey.

Shadow crouched, gauging the path to his heart. But somewhere in the muddled imprints of Ashi's brain, a city trick remained. Too fast to evade, his foot snapped out and the knife flew into the leaves. Death approached behind white eyes.

There had to be a way. The clarity. If she could see through his eyes, perhaps he could see through hers. An unpredictable course, but the only one at hand.

Even without Dorf's aid, the power came firmly here so close to the mountains. Shadow saw Ashi pause. His gaze met hers, tugging uncertainly as if to wrench out her soul. Instead of pulling away, she reached inside him. A flare of self-loss, and then she saw a bizarre landscape, all white, with a red figure that was herself.

A blood-longing fiercer than hunger throbbed through the body, a void sucking in its own fulfillment. She struggled against it, straining to pull her own awareness into Ashi.

With a jolt, whiteness dissipated into the night. Now he saw himself as she did, as Ashi, the innkeeper of the underworld, and for a moment he was himself again, a ghoul regaining its soul.

Yet there remained in him the sense-memory of a man's throat ripping away in his teeth, and the blood washing him, sating him. A wave of dark-brown horror grew in Ashi as he began to slip away from her, and Shadow staggered backward, her mind returning to her body.

With a howl, the man fumbled in the leaves and seized the knife. She cursed her own carelessness, and then he turned away and plunged the blade into his own chest. The eyes turned brown, then white, then brown, before he toppled.

Standing there, exhausted and stunned, Shadow began to realize how great a gift the clarity might be, greater even than she had realized. It had opened a channel between her and Ashi that had, for a moment, restored to a ghoul his own humanity. There might be many uses, for good or for evil, to which this talent could be put.

Leaving behind the crushed skull of his opponent, Dorf lumbered toward her, then stopped at the sight of Ashi lying dead with his hand still draped over the hilt of the knife. "What happened?"

"I'm not sure." Shadow pushed aside the hand and wrenched the knife from Ashi's chest, then wiped it on the ground. It was no use searching for other weapons; the Enforcers would have taken them. And now full night had fallen. They must find shelter.

A sense of ancient dust stopped her unexpectedly

as, out of the darkness with a fluid gray movement, a semicircle of menace formed about them.

Shadow braced her mind against the grayvers. She did not yet know the limits of the clarity, or whether it might hinder the Gray Ones. She would try Dorf's trick first and clear her mind.

But there was no assault. Instead, without any conscious intent, she began to walk forward, Dorf beside her. They had been commanded, in the subliminal manner of the grayvers. The things did not seek her soul, or they did not seek it here.

A short distance away, a slash opened in the earth. Shadow walked helplessly into it, instinctively shortening her stride to compensate for the slope. Within, there were neither ceiling nor walls, just a bizarre tube of rock that slanted downward, cold and glimmering with a whiteness so intense it bordered on yellow. The luminescence seemed to emanate from a brownish-green slime coating the walls.

Afterward, she had only an impression of stumbling down one corridor and then another, seeing passageways branch off in every direction. Beside her, Dorf clenched and unclenched his hands as if wishing for some solid foe.

They were descending, that much Shadow could tell. She could not, in the movement and confusion, concentrate on the clarity, yet she sensed an intelligence here, a purpose to their imprisonment. Taav had meant to explore the mountains. And then Hakin had made a bargain with someone, or something. The tribute was not given only to protect the city. What was it Briala had meant, when she said it was worth anything?

Slowly the light diminished. The smell of dankness and earth told her they had reached a dungeon. A section of wall, thick as a man's body, groaned open and stale air wafted out. Shadow willed herself to flee, but her legs carried her into the deep black cubicle. The door shuddered closed behind Dorf.

With no light to see by, Shadow pressed one hand against a wall and found it damp. They were deep within the mountain, shut away more hopelessly even than Nle. But for some purpose. She could only hope they would not be left here long.

As Shadow's eyes adjusted to the blackness she saw her friend silhouetted against the murk. The cell was not wide but long, unevenly shaped. "At least we have a little food—"

"Wait." Dorf turned toward the far corner of the cell, and then Shadow heard it, too, the soft sound of breathing.

There was something in here with them.

Chapter Six

Shadow caught hold of Dorf. She couldn't focus the clarity in her panic—and then their cellmate stepped close enough to be perceived with normal vision.

He was a chunky man, short, with wispy hair, almost buffoonish save for the assessing look in his eyes. His teeth were clamped around a stick attached to a tiny cup, which emitted a spicy smoke. Shadow's relief at finding him to be human quickly mutated into suspicion.

The man stared at her with distaste and something akin to amusement. "You?"

She fingered the hilt of her knife, wondering if his hefty pack concealed a weapon. Dorf shifted uneasily beside her. "You come from the city?"

"I've been there, yes." His gaze fixed on the top of her head. On the horns. "Ah. Not Briala, of course. You must be the one they call Mera-ti."

At the sound of her true name, she shivered; it had meant death to her these past dozen years. "I am called Shadow."

"And I am Lumle," the man said.

"How do you know of Mera-ti?"

"There was quite a disturbance in the city," he said. "Everyone heard of you."

"And what were you doing there?" From his smoking-rod, he was clearly a foreigner, and a brave one to have reached Ad-Omaq. He must hope to gain much, to take such a risk.

"I trade in this and that." While they spoke, Dorf had begun probing the walls for some way out, but Lumle shook his head. "Solid rock."

So he had examined the cell on his own, yet from the well-fed look of him, he hadn't been here long. Indeed, he couldn't have been, if he had visited the city so recently. Where he came from and what his mission was, there was no point in asking, for only a fool would tell the truth and this man was clearly no fool.

"There is always a way out." Shadow ran her hand over one of the rough stones as if it might hold some clue. "Even if it's only through the door." Suddenly, meaning to catch the stranger off guard, she said, "How do you know Briala?"

"I saw her at the ceremony, when she was elevated to ruler." He smiled a little at becoming the one to surprise.

"Ruler? When?"

"Two days after you left. The day Hakin died."

A sense of foreboding came over Shadow. Hakin had wanted to turn against the Gray Ones, and Briala had not. "That was sudden."

"Death usually is among leaders of the Radiants." He tapped bits of ash from his pipe.

Taav. He had been a young man. Shadow, a child, never questioned it. Had he been murdered? Had Hakin? "How did she die?"

"An illness, they said." Lumle pulled a pouch

from his cape, pinched out a shredded substance and tamped it into the cup, then produced a sparker of strange design, black interwoven with silver, hinting at faces in its depths. As he smoked, silence surrounded them, a deeper, more absolute silence than Shadow had ever known. She sat on a narrow ledge, feeling her breath come shallowly, as if the weight of the earth pressed on her shoulders. They had come far into the rock.

Beside her, Dorf seemed to feel the same oppression of spirit. "Shadow, why would they bring us here? Why not just—"

"Because of Ashi." She hesitated to say more, before this stranger.

"You used the clarity on him?" Dorf looked at her expectantly, not seeing that he had revealed more than she wished.

When Shadow didn't answer, Lumle asked, "And what might the clarity be?"

"A trick," she said shortly.

"The grayvers like tricks." He kept his pack close at hand as he sat on the floor, leaning against the wall. "I should have gone straight back to my ship, but no, I had to have a look around. I suppose it's a good thing the grayvers spotted me before the ghouls did. Maybe they think I have a few tricks they can steal, as well."

And probably he did, a foreigner who had come here by ship and kept close watch on events at the Citadel. "Such as blast-powder?" Shadow guessed.

The man shrugged. "I always carry a bit of this and that."

"How does it hurt them?" Shadow asked, her curiosity overcoming her dislike of appearing ignorant.

"Powder? It doesn't. Not directly." Lumle chewed

on the end of his smoke-rod. "But when they came out a while back—two, three hundred years ago—it drove them deep into their caves. Seems their strength is in the caverns, and when those are damaged, it weakens the grayvers."

"Is that why you're here?" Shadow challenged.

Lumle smiled, half to himself. "To blow up the caves? It would take more powder than would fit in this little pack. No, I assure you, being captured was none of my plan." He folded his arms across his chest and closed his eyes as if to sleep.

But she felt certain he was fully awake. Surviving in the city had taught Shadow to look beneath surfaces, and in this man she sensed much experience, much knowledge, and much purpose. So cunning a traveler must have seen many lands and many mysteries. He would not have come to Omaq without good reason, and he would not leave without learning all he could of it. Well, perhaps she could learn from him as well, but until she understood him better, she preferred to reveal as little as possible about herself.

Shadow made a bed on the floor. As she lay there, awake, she saw the foreigner watching her. Something he had said stuck in her mind. "You said the grayvers were driven back two or three hundred years ago. I thought it had been longer, a thousand years."

For a moment, she thought he wouldn't answer, and then he said, "So it has been, since they posed a serious problem. That was before the invention of blast-powder five hundred years ago. The last time they emerged, it drove them back without much trouble."

But this time, Hakin didn't have any, Shadow

recalled. Yet the grayvers had reappeared at least a year before the trade ban was imposed. "Why didn't the Radiants use it this time?"

"Apparently they underestimated the danger at first, and used up their stock blasting out more underground gardens. Or so they say." Lumle watched her closely as he spoke. Shadow sensed the information was a kind of trade, a way to learn more about her and her gift.

Perhaps he was a trader in blast-powder, a rogue who defied the trade ban. But Shadow felt something more in him than mere profit seeking.

She wished she remembered more of what Taav had told her about the world outside Omaq. She knew that centuries ago there had been wars, and afterward a council of many nations was established at Ad-Son to keep peace. It was the Council that had ordered the building of Ad-Omaq, against the wishes of the Kirite rulers, but Kir had accepted the Council's command. The new city had achieved its goal of bringing together the Radiants, allowing them to strengthen their special gift, the narrow-light, but instead of using it for good, they had thrown off Kir's yoke and the Council's as well, and made themselves tyrants and hedonists and tormenters of the old race.

Yet nowhere in this story did the Gray Ones figure. What was their role now, in the schemes of the Citadel?

There were other mysteries, too. "Before blast-powder was invented, when the grayvers came out, what finally stopped them?" Shadow asked. "Why didn't they overrun the land?"

"They did." Lumle took a deep breath, almost a yawn. "More than a thousand years ago, there was a great city near here, at the foot of the mountains.

The grayvers destroyed it; there's not a stone left. It seems that when there were no more souls to feed on, the Gray Ones returned to their caves."

Dorf sat up, as attentive as Shadow. "How do you know all this?"

"There is a library at Ad-Son." Lumle spoke as though it were the obvious thing to do, to consult the ancient books. Yet Ad-Son lay across the ocean. "Have I satisfied your curiosity enough for one evening?"

"That would be impossible," Shadow said.

The foreigner looked as though he might pose a question of his own, but then turned and seemed to sleep.

Although Dorf's breathing beside her soon became regular also, Shadow could not doze off so quickly. Taav had meant to explore the mountains. Had he stumbled across the grayvers? Did they have anything to do with his dying so young? The questions echoed through her mind, and through her dreams.

The scraping of the ponderous door woke her. Dim though it was, the light from the corridor gleamed in, bright by contrast with the cell. In the doorway hovered a gray robe shaped like a man. At its silent command, the three prisoners began the sloping journey upward, through the intensifying light that might have come from the mold layered upon the cave walls. Struck by the absence of warmth, Shadow pulled her cloak tighter.

Walking, they heard no sounds beyond their own footsteps and the distant drip of water. It would have been impossible to trace the twists and forks of their route through the blazing ivory tunnels, even had she wanted to.

A final turn and they stood in the entrance to a

vast hall that scalded her eyes with its whiteness. The roof was perhaps four times the height of a man; Shadow couldn't see the walls, although perhaps that was a trick of the curving floor and the blinding light. In the center, on a glowing silver throne, sat a tower of emptiness in a violet cloak.

Shadow felt the glacial power of winter and the destructive fury of death itself in the vast grayver which had become the Graylord. Instinctively, she feared him beyond anything she had ever encountered. Here was the vortex that had claimed thousands of souls, sucking them in through its subject grayvers and slavish ghouls.

She feared him not only as she feared cold and darkness and death, but in a deeper part of her that came from Mera. The Graylord was a creature of these mountains, and so was she. Whatever powers he held were linked in some perverted way to her own clarity. Why did the possibility burn at her that somehow, through her, he might find the pathway that would free him forever from this fastness and set him loose upon the world?

Shadow's attention was distracted by a pinkish mass seething around the base of the throne. It took a moment to identify it as a horde of naked people, chained and crawling over each other, livestock for the Graylord. She saw in their faces a terror so intense it stifled the will to live.

Shadow and her companions stepped forward, not of their own volition but of the Graylord's. As she looked directly at him, Shadow felt the clarity strengthen within her. She sensed many things: a great malevolent intelligence scanning her; a curiosity, touched with avidity; and something beyond that. A gathering of darkness, a restlessness to be on the move. As if she had stepped into the current of his mind, Shadow glimpsed fragments of thoughts eddying by: . . . *time for the harvest of bodies . . . they will be our moving caverns . . . south, south to Ad-Omaq . . . now that Briala rules . . .*

Then a voice spoke directly to her, in her mind, not in words and yet she understood it in words. *You have a power that was previously unknown to us. You have restored the soul to a ghoul. It is a talent that could be useful to us. Yes; more than useful.*

Beside her, Lumle turned in alarm. The voice, it appeared, had been audible not only to her. "Curses and Sajawak-fire, why didn't you tell me? Don't you see what this means?"

And she did see. That with the clarity, the Graylord could consume souls and bring them back again, could feed forever on the same victims, could grow so powerful that even blast-powder would not stop him. Even the forest of Kir, even the ocean might not be enough to hold him back.

"I—I have no such power." She strained to speak, hearing her voice echo thinly in the chamber.

Even the naked slaves ceased writhing as their master roared with a contempt that surged through Shadow's blood. *Do not lie to me. I will see for myself.*

He was pulling at her, taking her soul so swiftly and surely that no trick could even slow him. With a shock, the chill of the caverns penetrated Shadow's flesh as she felt her soul jerked from her body into the dark spaces of the Graylord, into an ice world where trees died beneath the winter white, and animals and people froze from within. Yet she was still herself, aware of her own separateness, not yet lost.

In a flash of insight, Shadow saw that at the end of

this glacial vision of the Graylord's lay a bizarre spring in which the desolate earth yielded up not saplings and flowers but fungus-forms and rotting, carnivorous plants whose roots fed on the decaying souls of the long-dead. Not only the people but the earth itself would die beneath his conquest.

And yet the Gray Ones must be part of the nature of Omaq, for they had sprung from the heart of the mountains themselves. If only she could grasp the essence of the things, perhaps Shadow could find a way to thwart them.

Her thoughts clouded. She was sinking into the morass of the Graylord. Lost; soon she would be lost.

Somewhere, outside this wasteland, the throne room still stood, and Dorf, and Lumle, and the body that had been Shadow's. She must retreat to it, must find a way or not only she and Nle but all things human would perish.

Nle. So many clever things he had told her, but it was to Dorf's trick that she turned now. With every fragment of concentration, she emptied herself, so that the mind of the Graylord met only a void—and then again she heard that laugh, hideous with triumph. *I am not fooled.* She was trapped here, fading . . .

Then the world erupted.

Rocks spewed from the roof of the cavern and the light of the walls flared away. With a roar of rage and pain, the Graylord spat out the sliver of light that was Shadow's soul. She staggered beneath the weight of her body, choking in the spore-filled dust, her head pounding with the screams of slaves.

Someone touched Shadow's shoulder. "Come quickly!" It was Lumle. "My blast-powder is gone, and the damage is less than it seems."

Chapter Seven

The three companions lurched over the rubble, coughing, clinging to each other. Shadow thought of the slaves, but in the dust and darkness dared not go back for them. She felt the Graylord searching for her.

Debris and flickering, uncertain light transformed the corridors into an eerie maze. Here and there the mold hung in tatters, providing only intermittent flashes of illumination. Strange stuff, it swayed lightly although there was no breeze and patches of it had already begun spreading across the newly bared walls. The caverns themselves were little damaged.

Their path led upward, Lumle plotting the way from one tunnel to the next. They saw no grayvers. The blast might have alarmed them, but Shadow sensed another reason. In a small chill space left from that momentary merging with the Graylord, she detected a massing of the grayvers, a compulsion to go south to Ad-Omaq, a drive that had begun before her arrival. Valuable as the clarity might be, the Graylord would not interrupt this—invasion.

But the grayvers had never gone far from the caves, not in recent times. Yet there had been ages, vast sweeps of time, dark and close in the heart of the mountain, for the Graylord to make his plan.

Taking souls expands the grayvers' strength, but its source lies in the caves. A phrase came back to her—*moving caverns.* What had the Graylord meant by that? What new scheme had he devised, and was it already too late to save Omaq, even with all the blast-powder in the world?

Shadow stumbled and nearly fell, and pulled her thoughts from the Graylord. Ahead of her, she saw a speck of sunlight, and hurried toward it. The way grew steeper and narrower. She and her companions crawled up the last stretch, emerging with a gasp into chilly dawnlight.

Lumle caught his breath in short rasps and led on, not directly down the mountain but on an angling course that took them behind boulders and brush. The clarity might have shown their pursuers, but it might also draw the Graylord, now that a channel had been opened between them.

The cool morning wind whipped away the heat from Shadow's skin as they climbed down a ravine. Below, an outcropping split the path, and Lumle started along the right-hand branch, southwest toward the Omaq River.

Shadow halted, with Dorf beside her. "We part here."

The foreigner stopped also. "Where do you go?"

"East."

"To Kir? Impossible." A rustling nearby made him turn sharply, but it was only a munt.

"What about you?" Dorf asked.

"South." Seeing the suspicion in Shadow's eyes, he relented enough to explain, "Not to the city. To the sea."

In the sneakways of Ad-Omaq, Shadow would have left him without another word. But here he was a friend, and she owed him for her life. "You won't survive to reach your ship, if you have one."

"Aye, if I still have one," he conceded. "You would take on the Mage, with this—clarity of yours?"

"Perhaps we're too small to concern him." Shadow pretended a confidence she didn't feel. "In the city did you hear of Nle, our friend in the dungeons? I'm going to seek help in Kir, any way I can." She said nothing of her concern for Omaq itself. Lumle might have saved her life, but it was too soon to know how far he might be trusted.

Lumle gave her a strange look. "There are forces at work of which you know nothing. But neither do they know anything of you. Very well. I will come." He reached into his pack, then uttered an oath. "Of all things to lose—my compass! Curses and Sajawak-fire! We'll have to steer by the sun."

And so they did, always with the sense of being followed although nothing could be seen or heard, and Shadow still feared to use the clarity. In a small space in her soul, she felt the Graylord moving, restless, voracious, his grayness cloaking the land-scape in mist, his evil touching her and falling across the world like a poisonous cloud.

Quickly, stealthily, Lumle led them through the ruins of old orchards, past long-abandoned farmhouses and bare, stark fields. Shadow remembered the rich-ness here, from her journey to Ad-Omaq a dozen years before, and shivered, thinking how soon after-ward the grayvers had come.

As evening traced long fingers across the land, she called upon the clarity at last, finding that it came

more sharply than ever before, and with it she saw
the Graylord's trap: a creeping circle of ghouls fanned
across the countryside, closing toward them. Soon
the dark would fall to shield the refugees from sight,
but not to hide the smell of their blood.

The things had not scented them yet, and the
circle was not perfect, might still be breached. But
Shadow's hopes shriveled as darkness lowered and
exhaustion dragged at her footsteps. The clarity showed
the ghouls closing in, dozens of them, urged on by
their own fierce hunger.

And then, somewhere ahead of them, a shriek tore
through the night. It might have been an animal, or
a child. Shouts followed, and heavy grunts. At their
backs, Shadow heard the panting of ghouls and knew
they had picked up the scent. There was no choice
but to run forward into whatever thrashed about, no
time even to use the clarity.

They burst through a stand of trees and into a
clearing where dark bodies twisted and struggled. In
the triple moonlight, there seemed to be hundreds
of them. Something was still screaming, screaming.
A harthorn lamb, tethered to a stake. The Graylord's
trap had closed on the wrong prey.

Migal's face appeared before her, caught by a cold
ray of moonlight. "Too many . . ." A ghoul seized
him, spun him around, slashing downward as Migal
thrust upward with his blade. They collapsed together, blood spurting into a single stream.

A hand caught Shadow's wrist. Dorf and Lumle
had vanished. Unable to reach her knife, she flipped
as Nle had taught her, the heel of her boot smashing
against the ghoul's chin. It crumpled, and she fell
from her own momentum, jarring her back. Around

her, bodies thudded and the lamb squealed until its voice cracked.

Then she heard another cry, high and desperate, not far off. The boy! Staggering to her feet, Shadow found him with the clarity, and hurled herself forward before the ghoul could strike him again. She clamped onto the fiend's back, bringing the knife down again and again, feeling flesh and muscle tear. The creature slumped. Frantically she shoved at its body until she found the boy beneath it. His throat gaped at her like a second mouth.

Shadow knelt, drained. After a time, she became aware of silence spreading over the field.

She lifted her head. Something stirred among the dark forms on the ground. Dorf, it was Dorf. She called out and he moved toward her wearily. Across the field, a white-eyed figure twitched out the last of its accursed life. Whatever other survivors there might have been had gone.

Lumle? Shadow found him with the clarity, untying the lamb's body. They met on the edge of the clearing and made camp a short distance away, risking a fire to roast the small animal, although Shadow had little appetite.

After they ate, Dorf dried the leftover meat to add to the small store of nuts and fruit in their packs. Without Lumle, Shadow would not have thought to retrieve the lamb; nor, she suspected, would any ordinary traveler. Without question this man had scouted and foraged before.

"If we're to go on together, I want the truth about you," she said.

"This clarity, as you call it—" Lumle lit his smoking-rod—"what can it do?"

So he insisted on the truth from her first. There

was no use in hiding it; he had already seen some of the clarity's workings for himself. "I don't know the whole of it myself." She leaned against the damp roughness of a tree. "It sees through the surface of things, puts me inside another's mind sometimes. That's how the ghoul came back—he saw himself through my eyes."

"You're a mixture of the old race and the new." The trader regarded her thoughtfully. "You gave a ghoul back its soul, if only for a moment. This gift might be deeper than you know."

"It opens channels." Shadow shuddered. "I still feel the Graylord's presence."

"Any powerful talent brings its own form of danger." Lumle spoke as if he had seen a great deal of the world and its gifts.

"I've answered your question," Shadow said. "And now, you. What were you doing in Ad-Omaq?"

"Speculating." The smoke from his rod was sweet, the smoke from the dying fire acrid. "There's money to be made in Ad-Omaq; lots of it, thanks to the Council's ban on trade."

"You defy them?"

"Not I." The foreigner laughed shortly. "No, my friend; I intend to live a long, wealthy, peaceable life. But you see, the Council wants Omaq to rejoin it, comply with its laws, share the Radiants' light-skills. And Kir wants Omaq as its province again. A half-dozen years ago, when the Mage learned the grayvers had returned, he asked the Council to recognize his sovereignty so he could battle them."

Lumle had been right. Shadow had known nothing of these matters: that the Mage had tried to retake Omaq, that the Council still existed, and that it knew of the grayvers' threat to Omaq. "Did the Council agree to let Kir rule?"

"Ah, no." Lumle sucked at his rod, though the spark within had died. "The Radiants would resist the Mage's dominance, and you know the strength of their weapons. The Council was established to keep peace, not stir up a devastating war. Instead, it ordered the forest closed, to force Ad-Omaq to rejoin the Council in order to get blast-powder."

So that was the reason for the trade ban. Of course, it was also possible that the trader was lying, but surely there was at least a hint of truth here, like a rare blue feather on a harkbird. "You've still not explained how there's money to be made."

"As you've seen for yourself, the Citadel is desperate and surely will soon come to terms." The foreigner appeared to take no offense at her challenge. "And if trade is restored, those who sell the blast-powder will do well indeed."

"So you came to assure your market. And did you?"

"I have left my message at the Citadel." Lumle stared into the fire. "What Briala will do—you may know as well as anyone."

"I know her not at all and trust her even less." Shadow thought of Migal and his fierce, proud band. Abandoned by their leaders. If she had been the legitimate daughter instead of Briala, Omaq would never have sunk to such depths.

Suddenly she felt the Graylord again, as if his name were an echo of Briala's. A gray cloud, heading south. But there were no words, only the strong impression that the Graylord himself was on the move.

"I'll stand guard." Dorf interrupted her thoughts.

Lumle reamed out his rod, tapping the ashes onto the hard ground. "Aye, and we'd better sleep while we can."

The awareness of the Graylord did not return that night, and a welcome haze of sleep brought Shadow's head down onto her arms. Her thoughts flew ahead, to the Forest of Kir. Bloodcats that leaped from nowhere, cliffs that tumbled away without warning. What manner of man was this Mage, who wanted to rule Omaq? He must have weaknesses. There must be a way through his forest. . . . She barely felt the blanket being laid across her shoulders as she drifted off to sleep.

She awoke to a thrum in the earth, a steady tramping that moved down from the mountains across the land. Wakefulness and awareness came in full, even as Lumle hissed a warning. The three of them lay silent, trusting to the cover of rocks and a gnarled tree half-smothered with vines. Pressed against the ground, she felt more than heard the army of the Graylord marching across the land. But what were these? It was vital to see them, to understand this new threat to Ad-Omaq and to the imprisoned Nle.

Touching Dorf, Shadow felt Lumle studying her intently as she drew on the clarity, but he quickly fell away from her mind as she pierced the distance between her and the . . . bodies. Yes, human bodies, but no longer alive—slaves from the Graylord's throne, peasants, even ghouls too weak to be of use—all dead. Yet they walked, and, driven by the Graylord's command, they were beyond stopping to hunt or feed. The words of the Graylord came back to her—moving caverns.

What was in these unnatural bodies? Whatever it

was, she knew with sudden, inexplicable certainty that the Graylord had devised a means that might, in time, place him beyond the power of blast-powder to halt.

And he wanted the clarity, the power to restore ghouls and feed on them again. He wanted Shadow.

She felt him grope toward her and nearly cried out. But someone was carrying her away, joltingly, breaking off the channel that linked her to the Graylord, and then she came back to herself and found she was slung over Dorf's shoulder and he was running.

"Wait," she gasped out, and Dorf lowered her onto shaky legs. "He's gone. The Graylord. You broke the contact." She shuddered and leaned against her friend.

She could no longer feel the walking dead; they must have moved on to the south. Lumle led the way east, wrapped in unshared thoughts, and so they passed that day and the next as the wintering days shortened. On the third night, their small fire burned like a beacon on a far shore, and Shadow drew close to Dorf. Even Lumle, although still an enigma, felt like a friend in these chill reaches.

"What do you know of the Mage?" Shadow asked at last. "They say he's powerful beyond measure."

The foreigner shrugged. "Powerful, yes. A strong ruler with a keen mind. But not beyond measure. He's a master of illusion. He can make you see and hear and smell what never was and never will be."

"Illusion and nothing more?" Shadow felt both relief and disappointment. "Then he couldn't help us rescue Nle, even if we reached him?"

"Don't weigh him lightly. He could rescue your

friend, if anyone could. In Kir, as in Omaq, great talents may be disguised as simple ones."

"And can he stop the grayvers, now that they've left their caverns?" Shadow demanded.

The small, round man looked at her with weary eyes. "I know too little of their nature to say. But I suspect if anyone can stand against them, it will be you."

Shadow pulled the blanket more tightly around her shoulders. "You saw how poorly I fared in the caves. Without you—"

"Your powers come from the old race of Omaq and from the Radiants. You are of this land; you may be tied to the grayvers in ancient ways unknown even to the Graylord. It might help if I knew more of this gift of yours. Can you touch my mind with it?"

Shadow hesitated. She had projected into the ormgrim's mind and Ashi's, but only in desperation. Yet perhaps the clarity was ready for this further test; it seemed to have strengthened these past weeks. "You really think it's necessary?"

"I must know, if I am to report—" Lumle stopped himself. "In this matter, I must ask for your trust. There are things I dare not reveal even to you."

Shadow had long suspected, or perhaps merely hoped, that her gift might somehow be linked to the fate of Omaq. So far she had stumbled blindly along, using the clarity as chance dictated. Now, perhaps, it was time to turn to someone more knowledgeable, although what Lumle's true mission was, she could not yet guess. "All right."

She faced Lumle across the fire, and concentrated. There was a blank space, a barrier, and then a sudden rushing in. She saw a village by the sea, fishing ships with single masts, cottages crowding together along the docks. She heard a blur of alien voices and saw a girl smile. Home.

Beyond that, she received a jumble of impressions: dancers in bright feathers; perfumed air; a beaked creature with seven legs that transformed itself into a man in a burst of smoke; a vast staircase carved into the stone of a cliff, covered with tiny people and animals winding past each other; and again the smell of the ocean, full of salt and distances.

Shadow drew back into herself. She had confirmed that Lumle was a seafaring traveler, a man of many experiences, but she still knew nothing of his purpose. He had managed to hide that much even from the clarity.

Lumle was breathing hard, the fire casting angry shadows on his face. "Damn bloodcat." He rubbed his shoulder, looking startled when his fingers found no wound. How much of Shadow's past had he experienced? "I've encountered nothing like this before." The foreigner smiled a little, and stretched. "Thank you, Mera-ti."

Staring into the fire, Shadow reflected that each day seemed to reveal some new aspect of the clarity. The sounds and smells of Lumle's village still seemed real to her, as if they were her own memories. She could even understand the foreign words, what few she remembered.

She just hoped Lumle hadn't taken away more than she had gained from the exchange.

The next day they reached the forest. From morning, they could spy it as a dark line on the horizon. Coming closer, up a swell of the land, Shadow made out the great trees, arching disdainfully away from the thin line of a path, their many-hued leaves rustling in speechlike rhythms. An ominous refuge, the

Mage's land. Barred by the ruler of Kir, and now, Shadow saw, by the Graylord himself.

For, just outside the forest, white-eyed ghouls patrolled in an unending line. Omaq itself had become a prison.

Chapter Eight

Surprisingly, it was Dorf who stilled the panic in Shadow's heart. "They're not real. I can't hear them."

Shadow closed her eyes to concentrate on the clarity. The day was brisk with afternoon, and warmer than it had been. She smelled the grass beneath her, felt the sun on her back and heard the soft breathing of the two men. Ahead lay the upslope of land and the Forest of Kir, its trees muttering among themselves.

There were no ghouls. "He's right," she said, releasing the clarity. "They're illusions."

"Well, I'll be *slevjak*," Lumle said, and Shadow wondered what that meant. "He had me fooled, and I thought I was prepared."

They ventured forward, still hardly daring to believe the ghouls that looked so real were nothing but air. Shadow walked within inches of one and put her hand through it.

Illusions were not unknown in Ad-Omaq; from Kir, traders had brought small figures, fantastic images without substance and yet permanently shaped, for the games of Highborn children. They were worked, so Nle had said, with the image-talents of

Kirite artisans just as the Radiant artisans made lamps that could glow with their own power. But this vast creation of the Mage's indicated a talent that went far beyond the making of toys. As Lumle had implied, it seemed that the clever use of illusions could be turned into a powerful weapon.

The three of them funneled onto the narrow path. A warm dampness met them. This was an old forest, long undisturbed. One might, Shadow felt, use the clarity to catch a glimpse of ages past. But when she tried, she saw only the trees. Her clarity did not yet encompass such strengths.

Besides, there was enough danger in the here and now to concern Shadow. She did not like this cramped threading of their way. *Never enter an alley if you can't see the way out,* Nle had said.

An overpowering sweetness spewed up with every step from the small white starflowers that carpeted the path, obscuring the senses, clouding the mind. Translucent leaves of blue-green, red and gold refracted the light overhead, scattering crisscrossed shapes onto the ground that dizzied and disoriented her.

Shadow had expected, without realizing it, that once out of Omaq her spirits would lift. Instead, a sense of being watched pressed down upon her. She had left the reach of the Graylord for the realm of the Mage. That he was a man, she knew from Taav's description, but certainly he was not a welcoming one.

As they walked, Lumle cast his rod and smoking-pouches to the ground. Shadow wondered what they revealed, that he did not want to take them to Kir. If only the clarity could penetrate the silent spaces within Lumle's mind. Whatever his secrets, he might endanger Shadow and Dorf, or they might unwittingly endanger him.

"How far is it to Ad-Kir?" Dorf's simple question drew her back to the present.

"As far as the trail wants to take us," Lumle said. "They don't run straight, and it's said each is different."

Could all these defenses be illusory! And if the Mage, with his great powers, piled illusion upon illusion, would the clarity be able to penetrate them all? Shadow, watching the strange leaf-lights shift across the woods ahead of her, sensed a devious intelligence piercing the forest, entering the hearts of intruders and twisting what it found there against them.

Yet for a time they encountered no opposition, although the path remained narrow and unyielding. Sometimes Shadow thought she understood a few words of the tree murmurings—*Haseelon*. Strangers. *Seewheeah*. Horns. Her hand brushed over her head instinctively; and at the same time, she remembered Mera bending over the plants that grew along a stream, knowing instinctively which were poisonous and which could heal. Perhaps she had heard their language although, if so, she had not spoken of it.

Shadow was grateful that, here in the forest, no more sense of the Graylord stretched toward her. Yet a small chill curled in a corner of her soul, and waited.

Twilight sank rapidly upon them. Wearily, Shadow stretched her shoulders. The hours of fruitless watching had dulled her awareness.

The bloodcat flashed around a bend in the trail, a stray beam of light glittering on its blind, ruby eyes. There was nowhere to flee. Overhead, the trees lifted their branches away, denying refuge, as the beast uttered its chilling keen. Instinct cried out for flight, but Shadow drew her knife and advanced. Again the snarl came, hungry and triumphant. Strange how its attention seemed to focus past her and on Lumle.

Or—not on Lumle, but on where he stood. Shadow drew on the clarity and saw only the trees.

"Illusion." She tucked the knife away. The blood still pounded through her body, fear-quickened. "I should have been more alert. Let's make camp."

Down a slope they found a stream and a small clearing, perhaps once used by caravans. They dared gather only a handful of dead branches in the hostile darkness, and made a thin meal of a fish Lumle caught, roasting it over the fire. The wizardwood burned white, glowing at its core. *A white chamber, a gray mist, an inner eye that probed and pulled at her.* Shadow jerked her thoughts away and turned to Lumle. "What did you mean by *slevjak*?"

"Part of the Symmetry of Six," the foreigner said.

"And what is that?" Shadow watched as a dark shape passed overhead against one of the moons, but it was only a night-flying bird.

"In Kir, the Symmetry of Six denotes the categories of relationships between men and women. Ad-Kir isn't the product of a single culture, but of many, and such things must be defined."

Shadow thought of Omaq. A Radiant woman had power of her own; a peasant or a Highborn might marry and be protected by her husband; any other must fight or have defenders, or she would find herself enslaved in the Street of Lost Women. "What are these categories?"

"In Ad-Kir, it violates the law to take a woman against her will." Lumle groped inside his robe and then frowned as his hand met emptiness instead of a rod. "*Slevjak* is the briefest of contacts. *Farraja* is the highest, true marriage; but the Kirites would not call the one high, or the other low."

"And the other four?"

"After *slevjak*, there's *mlevja*—a relationship in trade, which may last a day, a month, however long it takes to fulfill the bargain. Then *shohaja*, also of moderate duration, entered into for pleasure. *Cohaja* is the same, but the couple may live together for years. The last is *reqaja*, a marriage of state, but there has been none of these as long as anyone can remember."

A strange land, Kir, Shadow reflected as she lay inhaling the scent of the crushed flowers. A woman could not be taken against her will. The Mage might be cruel and cunning, yet he ruled his own people kindly. More kindly, at least, than Taav. When at last Shadow slept, she dreamed of her mother's cottage and Taav's easy smiles, dreams that she woke with the memory of in the morning.

The next day they proceeded with caution. The clarity showed the stream to be much deeper than it looked, and they had to leap rather than ford it. Shadow wished she dared use the clarity at all times, but knew it would exhaust her.

Still, she used it frequently although there was no sign of danger, and by midday felt more than usually drained. And uneasy. The trail curved and doubled back, so that one lost all sense of direction, and the trees blocked the sun. Where the trail led was impossible to tell. They might be going in circles, or doubling back, for all she knew.

They stopped only briefly for lunch, and by mid-afternoon the strain became almost overwhelming.

Shadow walked unsteadily, and the clarity was blurred when she used it. Still, she forced herself to keep going. Nle had little time left; each hour was precious.

Then, as the forest darkened, they emerged into open land. Shadow sank back against Dorf. They had indeed made a semicircle, one that carried them some distance to the south. The towers of Ad-Omaq were plainly visible, evening gloom gathering above the white walls of the Citadel. As they watched, the gate drew open and a small band of men marched out, shackled together, Enforcer-guarded. Even at this distance, Nle stood out, his figure slight among the burly men.

Shadow pushed forward, her weariness gone. The Graylord's army of lurching bodies must be near. Surely the Enforcers would turn aside when she told them that the grayvers were attacking. The treaty was broken, so there was no reason for tribute now, no reason to sacrifice Nle. . . .

"No!" Dorf's hands clamped around her shoulders, checking her forward rush. Shadow strained against him, but her friend tightened his hold. "No, it's wrong. It's too soon for the tribute."

"The forest doesn't come this close to the city," Lumle said.

Shadow quieted. With the clarity, she witnessed the trap the Mage of Kir had laid. There was no open land, no city, and no tribute. She had veered from the trail and was about to step into an open pit. A soft slither from the bottom warned of what coiled there, the same death that had met the bloodcat in the sewers.

"Aka-serpents." There were bones jumbled together in the pit. Shadow cursed the Mage and turned back to the path.

They put an hour's distance between themselves and that horror before making camp at a clearing Shadow inspected carefully. There was no treachery, but also no food or water, and their supplies were dwindling.

After a meager dinner, Shadow lay down to sleep. Had it not been for Dorf, slow, plain-thinking Dorf, she would have died. Perhaps the ability to think simply was a kind of clarity in its own right. In the city, where the slowness of a peasant might condemn him to servitude, she had thought the countrymen ill-made, little better than beasts. Now she saw that their very lack of quickness might be a useful adaptation.

The next day the travelers reluctantly agreed that Shadow must use her skill at all times. The illusions appeared to grow more deadly, the closer they came to their destination.

The bones in the serpent pit testified that others had come this far, perhaps members of the old race or desperate peasants or even Radiants who had quarreled with Hakin. The Mage had surely left his finest traps for last.

So the trio moved slowly over the next two days, allowing Shadow frequent rest. The two men described where the path appeared to turn to the right, and Shadow saw it would have dropped them into a great cleft in the earth. Lumle and Dorf pointed out as well where a fierce fire blocked the way, and where an ormgrim fed on the body of a woman and turned its evil attention to them as they approached. Shadow neither saw nor heard any of these.

They found no more food, and soon had none left in their packs. Still Shadow kept up her difficult guarding, while Lumle pocketed several sharp stones in case any game crossed their path.

By evening, hunger had become a fourth companion. It was with relief that they saw a small harthorn leap into view, and Shadow determined that it was real. One of Lumle's stones smashed into the beast, and it fell lifeless. The three of them hurled themselves forward.

Something snapped in the air. Netting closed around Shadow, jerking her from her feet. Nearby Dorf and Lumle dangled, each imprisoned in his own mesh snare.

"Sajawak-fire!" Lumle twisted around to pull his sparker from his pack. "How could we step into a common trap?"

The Mage, Shadow saw, knew better than any of them the uses of simplicity.

The netting, they found, could not be burned, nor did it yield to the knife, and struggling only made the web tighten. So Shadow hung there beside her friends, hungry and beginning to be afraid, as night came.

Chapter Nine

Enforcers cut them down in the morning. The five men wore unfamiliar uniforms, dark green with tubes for the arms and legs. Their leader, addressed by the others as Vank, supervised the operation with cold indifference, until he found the smoking-rod in Dorf's robe.

"You are not from Omaq." He held the rod carefully, as though it were a weapon. "This is an outlander's possession."

"I found it in the forest," Dorf said stubbornly. Shadow, standing behind him, could see his large hands tremble. He must have meant to save it as a favor to Lumle, and now they would all pay the price.

"Bind them."

Rough hands thrust Shadow's arms before her and wrapped cord around the wrists, cutting the skin. "Are you the Mage's men?" she demanded.

The Enforcer ignored her, turning to Lumle. "How did you get through the forest?"

Lumle blinked and said blandly, "We walked."

"Then you shall walk to the palace, and await the Mage's pleasure." At a command, the Enforcers shoved them forward, southeast toward the sea. Stiff, hungry, uneasy over what lay ahead, Shadow plodded along, scarcely noticing how much warmer it was here than in Omaq.

They descended from the forest. Below them spread Ad-Kir. Its low buildings glistened in the sun, their walls the colors of the sea, blue and green, so that one could hardly tell where the land ended and the water began.

Beyond the buildings lay the harbor, the fabled port, pearl-winged ships clustering together like feeding birds. The air smelled of brine and sweat, spices and lumber; and Shadow could hear, faintly, the shouts of the stevedores. She remembered, as from her own experience, Lumle's fishing village and the feathered dancers and the shape-changer. From Ad-Kir, one could journey anywhere, to Kirrillea and Exsena, Sajawak and Son, the lands Taav had yearned to visit but never reached. If Nle were with them—but even then, how could she sail away forever? Omaq must be saved, as much from the Radiants as from the grayvers.

The rutted path gave way to a road with flat white stones. Square white houses lined the street, with flowers in the yards and children who watched unafraid as the strangers passed. One boy made illusions in the air, small translucent shapes of trees and ships that popped like bubbles.

Then the houses became taller and were set closer together, casting shadows in the street. It was impossible now to see the harbor, but the smell of the sea was everywhere. At last the buildings opened into a plaza, a marketplace bright with booths and blankets, with jewelry and cloth, arrays of orange and yellow fruit, braziers roasting strips of meat that made the emptiness swell in Shadow's stomach. People turned and glanced at them, but without great interest, for there were all manner of folk here, in tubed garments and robes, heavy brocades and airy silks, their perfumes eddying among the cooking smells. Great horns curled from a woman's head; a man's dark skin was tinged with blue; and voices chattered through the air in a dozen languages, like the surge of the ocean.

They left the market behind and approached the palace, its ivory walls shot with blue and yellow and rose. Within, a fountain splashed in the center of a flower-circled courtyard where Vank ordered them to wait. Shadow's mouth tasted of dust.

A group of women strolled from an arched doorway. Seeing the prisoners, they paused, except for a girl about Shadow's age with long white hair and pale blue eyes. Pushing past a large, stern-faced woman, she scooped a dipper from the fountain and brought it to Shadow. It was cold, from a deep well.

"Majia Silla!" The large woman stalked toward the girl. "Come away!"

"Why, Greda?" The girl darted back with water for Lumle and Dorf, pushing past an Enforcer. "You can see they're tied. They can't harm me. And they may amuse us. It's so dull here!"

The woman caught her charge by the wrist. "You know nothing of their powers. Think what it would do to your parents or your uncle if any harm came to you."

"At least let me talk to them!" the girl demanded, resisting.

Greda hesitated. The girl was smaller then Greda, but was too strong to be dragged away easily. "You may speak to them for a moment, if it will calm you."

The girl turned quickly to Shadow. "Who are you? Where do you come from?"

"Omaq."

"You're very dirty." The girl wrinkled her nose. "They can't see my uncle like that, can they, Greda?"

"We were ordered to wait, Majia Silla," one of the Enforcers said.

"Oh, never mind what Vank says." Silla turned to Greda. "What would Uncle Kirji say? I can smell them from here!"

Vank returned. The Mage was not ready to interview the prisoners, he said; and yes, they could be bathed. Silla smiled triumphantly at Greda, as though she had won her point. Shadow kept silent, disliking the girl's arrogance. Yet the water had been welcome. And the Mage's niece might prove even more helpful in other ways.

The guards herded the prisoners down a column-lined walkway. Two women in green uniforms took Shadow to a room with a tiled floor and a tub of hot water. She resented the need to stand naked before them, but the filth of the journey displeased her so she threw off her soiled robe and mud-caked boots and made herself clean, not looking at them, acting as though they were servants. Afterward they dressed her in a blue garment, also with tubes for arms and legs.

"Who are Majia Silla's parents?" she asked as she brushed out her hair.

"The Mage's sister, the Lady Fia, and her husband, the Lord Chamberlain," said one of the women. "Now come, if you wish to eat."

In an adjacent courtyard, they gave her pastries with spiced chopped meat and flat round bread spread with a tan, nutty paste. With the meal came Silla, alone, dashing into the courtyard and pausing for a moment with the sunlight behind her, white hair glowing around her face. A beautiful young woman, but one who knew it too well.

"Where is Greda?" demanded one of the Enforcers. "She is your guardian until your parents return from Ad-Son."

"She told me to stay in my room." The girl shrugged. "If you let me talk a little, I'll go away."

"A word or two. Your uncle will be ready soon."

Silla turned her attention to Shadow. "You're pretty. You should smile at my uncle, if you know how to smile; are you always so solemn? Offer *mlevja* to him, in trade for your freedom. It would be fun to see him with a foreigner. He's never done that."

"What are your parents doing in Ad-Son?"

The girl waved a hand as if it were a matter of little importance. "The Council is meeting. To determine the fate of Omaq."

"By what right?" Shadow demanded.

"Omaq is ours, of course." Silla nibbled at one of the pastries, then threw the rest to some fantailed birds that pecked in the yard. "I'm to inherit it, unless Kirji marries, of course. But I doubt he will. Who would he marry? He's never gone beyond *shohaja*, and hardly ever that."

"This Council meeting. Why—"

Vank came into the courtyard, frowned at seeing Silla, and spoke harshly to one of the women Enforcers. They led Shadow away, to the front of a domed white building, where Dorf and Lumle waited. Dressed in Kirite clothing, they made a strange-looking pair, the one large and slow-moving, the other short and crafty.

Vank signaled them to enter through an arched

doorway. To Shadow's surprise, the Enforcers stayed behind.

"Watch what you say," Lumle murmured as the three of them walked inside. "We may be observed." From his slight headshake, Shadow gathered she should not question him.

They passed through a small antechamber, high-ceilinged and echoing with their footsteps, and into a long plain room with arch-topped windows and unpadded wizardwood benches. In the center, a table ran almost the length of the room.

Dorf pointed to it. "It's a little world!"

Following his gaze, Shadow saw that the table was covered with tiny sculpted mountains and valleys, miniature trees that swayed as if in a wind, farms and cities. The oceans shimmered and flowed, and tiny people turned the earth with their plows, sailed the ships, thronged the markets of the cities. It took a minute for Shadow to recognize the curve of the coast, the rambling edges of the forest and the white tower of the Citadel. Here were the Eastern Lands in miniature, as vibrant as life.

"Does it please you? It is the work of some years." Where had he come from, this silver-haired man who stood beside Dorf? Of average height and slender build, the Mage of Kir wore a simple black garment and from his face and manner was in his thirties, despite the color of his hair. "It's only illusion, of course. But it endures. In the library at Ad-Son—but perhaps you have been there?"

"We're from Omaq," Dorf said.

"And this?" In Kirji's hand appeared a pouch—an illusion, but it smelled like Lumle's smoking-rod. "An exotic scent, from Kirrillea, perhaps?"

"It isn't mine," Dorf said. "I found it."

"Ah, yes. In the forest." The Mage opened the pouch and examined the contents. "Very fresh. Left there not long before you passed. A curious coincidence." The pouch vanished.

"It's mine," Lumle's jaw twitched.

"Ah." The Mage's turquoise eyes, unnervingly bright against his pale hair, fixed on Lumle. "And who or what might you be?"

"A messenger for the Council." He didn't meet Shadow's eyes. So that was what Lumle had been hiding. She might not have trusted him so much had she known, and no doubt he had anticipated that.

"And a spy, too, I'll warrant," said the Mage.

"Aye, that, too."

The two men faced each other assessingly, and yet Shadow had the odd sensation that they watched her as well, without seeming to.

"And have you come here with a message for me? Or to spy on me?" Kirji asked.

With only a blink of hesitation, Lumle said, "I can tell you this much: I was sent to Ad-Omaq with a message for the Radiants, asking their terms to rejoin the Council. I—was unable to reach my ship, and so I came here."

"How fortunate that you found such pleasant companions along the way." The Mage did not move, yet Shadow felt as if he circled them, closing in. "Let me see if I understand. Missing your ship, you naturally decided to come to the port at Ad-Kir. On the way, you met two other travelers, also bound for Kir, and so you came together."

Lumle said nothing. It was obvious to them all that no such thing could have occurred; the forest was closed.

"Sad to report, no ship has arrived here from the

Council, nor have there been inquiries made for
you," the Mage went on. "Perhaps it went back to
Ad-Son. But never mind. You will stay here as my
guests. After my sister and her husband return, a
way may be found to transport you to the Council."
He turned as if to leave.

There was more here than Shadow could grasp,
some undercurrent running between the Mage and
the messenger. As she considered how to broach
Nle's plight and their need to return to Ad-Omaq,
Lumle spoke again. "I cannot wait, Lord Mage. I
must have passage immediately. I can arrange it
myself, with some trader or other."

"Why such haste? You have had a long journey. I
insist that you stay a while." The Mage dropped the
words carefully, like a snare, and waited.

"I must report to the Council at once."

"With the Radiants' reply? But you have left a
message-bird with them, have you not? It will deliver the answer itself. And what other report could
there be?" Without warning, the Mage's hand brushed
across the top of Shadow's head, against the soft skin
of her horns. "Has it anything to do with this? Horns
and yellow eyes. Not an ordinary combination, I
think."

He knew who she was; somehow, the Mage had
heard of Mera-ti. If the Council had spies in Ad-
Omaq, so must Kirji. Now Shadow understood: that
in his report, Lumle meant to tell of her gift and to tell
them she had a claim to be ruler of Omaq. And she
saw that the Mage would prevent such a report, so
the Council would grant sovereignty to him instead.

"The Council will be angry," Lumle began.

"They will have no reason. In my storehouses

there is blast-powder enough for the grayvers, and I can manage the Radiants better than this—outcast."

"Your blast-powder may not be enough." Shadow's words brought the turquoise eyes to bear on her with a flicker of surprise, as if the wall had spoken. "The grayvers are marching against Ad-Omaq."

"Their power lies in the caves." The Mage dismissed her with the turn of his head.

"Not any longer!" Anger sharpened her voice. "How they've done it, I don't understand yet, but they've taken their power with them, or some of it."

"And how do you know this?" He turned to face her.

"I have a gift, a certain way of seeing through things." Shadow wondered how much she dared reveal. "I saw through your illusions; that's how we penetrated the forest. And I've touched the Graylord's mind."

"And you know how to defeat him?"

"Not yet," she admitted.

"As I thought." He stepped back, indicating that the interview was at an end. "You are my guests here until my sister returns. But, of course, you may not leave the palace without my permission."

Before Shadow could speak again, he vanished.

Chapter Ten

"Is he still here?" Lumle asked quietly.

Shadow concentrated, and saw the Mage in a corner of the room, cloaked by the illusion of invisibility. He must have seen the way she looked at him, for he turned and left. "He's gone now."

"Are we prisoners?" The proceedings clearly had confused Dorf.

"Officially, no. But, yes, we are." Lumle reached instinctively into his robe for the smoking-rod and grimaced as he withdrew his hand, empty. "Could at least have given the cursed thing back, couldn't he?"

A grayness tugged at Shadow's brain, an unexpected glimpse of the Graylord's mind. She hadn't thought the channel could reach so far. *The bodies can wait now, so near the city. The time is close. No need to face the light-weapons. Briala . . .*

"Briala?" Shadow said aloud, without realizing it, and the sound of her own voice drew her back. "The Graylord. He's outside Ad-Omaq. His plan—it concerns Briala somehow." She was beginning to see that this new path opened by the clarity might be of some benefit, at least provide some information, but the contact frightened her nevertheless.

"If he isn't in the city yet, Nle might still be safe," Dorf pointed out.

"These are urgent matters." Lumle stared out one of the windows into a courtyard where servants were setting up tables filled with food beneath a canopy. "I must reach the Council. They know nothing of you, Shadow. Whatever message Briala has sent is surely deceptive, if she answered them at all. Curses and Sajawak-fire! I knew the Mage wanted to regain Omaq, but I never believed he would be blinded by self-interest."

Shadow took a deep breath. "I must persuade the Mage to help me. I need a mantle of invisibility to get back to Ad-Omaq." It might not deceive the ghouls or bloodcats, unless he could hide her blood-scent as well, but it was the Radiants that Shadow feared most. Above all, her sister. Shadow's birth made her a threat so long as they both lived.

"You won't yield your claim to rule to win the Mage's help in freeing your friend?" Lumle demanded. Clearly he had chosen to take her side, and his support strengthened Shadow's resolve. Not only because he was an agent of the Council but because she could see that Lumle knew much of the mysteries of the world, of its ebb and flow and currents. He believed as she did that the clarity had a purpose of its own.

"No. It isn't only for Nle's sake that I'm going back. The people deserve better than to be slaves of the Radiants or the Mage." Shadow squared her shoulders. "I must find a way to persuade him." And with a murmur of farewell, she went in search of Silla.

A servant guided her to the women's quarters, where Shadow's few belongings had been placed in an airy bedchamber tiled in shades of blue. Several Kirite garments hung in an open wardrobe.

"The Majia Silla will come to you here, if she wishes," said the servant, and withdrew.

Shadow felt strange being in this room, as if she had entered it to thieve. Yet there was little here to steal, so simply and cleanly was the palace designed in contrast to the Citadel. No glittery Radiant-made baubles lay strewn about—necklaces that shone with their own light, or globes of dancing colors. There was only a firm bed covered with soft fabric, a deep blue carpet upon the floor, and a mirror-backed table.

Shadow sat before the mirror, regarding a face she scarcely recognized as her own. It was older than she remembered, the face of a young woman and not a girl. Unexpectedly, Kirji intruded into her thoughts, his gaze probing her. Not in the manner of Argen or Migal, yet he had been aware of her in all ways.

A curtain swished open to reveal Silla. "Well, what did you think of my uncle?" She stopped behind Shadow and smiled for the mirror.

"What did he think of me?" Shadow returned, for she had no doubt Silla had come here with her uncle's permission. Perhaps at his prompting.

"Oh—that you're a strange one." Silla examined the oddments of Shadow's pack, which someone had spread out on a bench. "Are these all the clothes you have? And you the daughter of Taav?"

"What else did your uncle say?"

"He's curious, of course. No one else has ever gotten through the forest. I'm sure he'd like some—demonstration." There was nothing subtle about Silla. Shadow wondered if the Mage knew how transparently she revealed his wishes, and concluded that surely he did.

"It might be arranged." She debated how much to disclose, knowing it would reach the ears of the Mage. There was no point in revealing that she intended to oppose him for the leadership of Omaq, if she ever got the chance. The rescue of Nle was enough of a reason to return to Ad-Omaq. "I need a favor, a small thing from him. . . ."

"The illusion of beauty? But you're pretty enough without that. Wealth, perhaps?"

"Invisibility." Shadow told her briefly of Nle's plight. "I want to get him out."

Silla only half-listened, as if the subject were dull, but at the end she clapped her hands together childishly and said, "I have it! You can challenge him. He loves games—illusion matches. They're very popular here."

"I'm sure he always wins." There were games in Ad-Omaq as well, but among the thieves and slavers they were vicious affairs, with the rules made up as they went, and likely ending in a fight. She did not think the Mage would play so crudely. His illusions could be very subtle.

"Of course he's accustomed to winning, but that's what's so exciting about it!" Silla perched on the edge of the bed. "You could see through his illusions. He wouldn't know what to expect—he might even lose!"

If he had considered that possible, Shadow thought, would he have instructed Silla to suggest it? "What are these games like?"

"Oh, there are judges, and the challengers agree on the rules." Silla appeared impatient with such details. "It might be who can create the most beautiful bird, or they might stage a battle with illusion-soldiers; whatever they're in the mood for."

A game. It was wrong that Nle's life and perhaps the future of a nation must be staked on such frivolity, an entertainment for Highborns like Silla. And what could Shadow wager, in exchange for what she wanted?

"I will think about it," Shadow said.

The jangle of bells entered her thoughts, musical tones echoing across the courtyards and chambers, announcing the evening meal. Silla went out, not even saying good-bye, and a servant arrived to guide Shadow.

The people of the palace dined together, servants and lords alike, selecting their food from an array spread along tables in a courtyard open to the evening sky. The food was elaborate, nutty paste molded into the shape of a bird, harthorn meat thinly sliced and pinwheeled. From long habit, Shadow took as much as she could fit on her plate.

She found Dorf and Lumle together at a table, speaking quietly. Focusing, Shadow saw a third figure beside her friends. Greeting them, she added loudly, "And will you not join us, my lord?"

Others in the courtyard turned to stare as the Mage appeared. He smiled in an odd way and walked off to the food table. From where he sat, the Enforcer Vank glared at Shadow as if resenting the fact that she had embarrassed his lord. Silla, standing with a group of friends, whispered to a curly-haired youth beside her, and they laughed.

Nibbling at a round of bread spread with paste, Shadow told her friends what Silla had said. "I suppose there's no choice; I'll have to do it. But what can I offer him?"

"You won't lose, so it doesn't matter," Dorf said loyally.

Lumle looked less confident. "You'll have to leave it up to him, I suppose. But do not be tricked into yielding your claim to Omaq."

Twilight was giving way to night, and across the palace globes shone forth, dispelling the darkness. Not all had been purchased from Omaq before the trade ban, Lumle explained; some were made in Kir by Radiants who had fled their homeland when Hakin came to power. Here, he said, they were accepted, so long as they made no attempt to interfere with Kirji's rule.

Now that his mission had been revealed, he spoke more freely of what he knew and had been. A fisherman by birth, an adventurer by nature, in his youth Lumle had traveled from his home village of Peh-Lenk to Ad-Son and been glad of the chance to work for the Council, for they sent him to many lands. In Kirrillea, where the mystic scent-dancers worked their magic, he had lain with a woman, and tried in vain to prevent her ritual suicide a year later at the coupling of the three moons. He had taken their infant daughter home with him to be raised by his mother in Peh-Lenk. The child, he said, was almost grown now, and was a little like Shadow in spirit.

That night Shadow dreamed of the three moons. They seemed to move willfully about the sky, and each had a face. At first she recognized men from the Den of Ashi, but then she saw that one of the faces was Taav's. The second was Hakin's. The third shed an evil white glow that she knew came from the Graylord. It swelled, pulling the other two into its aura and casting its light toward the earth. Searching, searching. Shadow fled through a forest, but the trees swayed away, revealing her path. The Graylord's cold breath chilled across her and she awoke on the edge of a scream.

The day was gray and overcast. Shadow dressed carefully, choosing a lavender garment and allowing a servant to brush out her hair.

Directed to the Mage in his illusion-garden, Shadow entered through a side gate. There were blossoms here that never existed in life: giant striped petals framing ripples of scarlet lace, soft white clouds billowing from a violet stem, and, most startling of all, a row of brown and yellow flower-faces that turned to watch as she passed. The Mage no doubt had been told of her coming, yet he stood with his back to her, concentrating on a tiny pink bloom that filled the air with honeyed sweetness.

Shadow stood silent, unwilling to beg for his attention. The contest between them had begun the moment she entered the forest and would not end until the fate of Omaq was decided.

At last the Mage turned. "Welcome to my garden."

"You know why I come."

"To propose a match; but I do not know what the stakes may be." He smiled a little, though, as if she were about to step into a trap.

"I need the illusion of invisibility for myself and for Dorf so we can rescue a friend from the Citadel." She watched closely, trying to read whether he believed her explanation.

"You would go back, at risk of your life?" He was a master at keeping his face clear of emotion. "To reach a friend, you say?"

"More than a friend. A brother in spirit." Shadow spoke sharply. She was not accustomed to such devious mental maneuvering, and it annoyed her.

The Mage turned away, pretending interest in his

flower scents, but Shadow knew he was weighing her offer.

"These are my terms," he said at last. "That I have one hour to trick you, to produce an illusion you cannot see through, to the satisfaction of the judges."

"And what prize do you demand, if you win?"

He shrugged as if it scarcely mattered. "One week of *mlevja.*"

Mlevja. A relationship given in trade. At least he hadn't demanded she relinquish her claim to rule Omaq. "I need time to consider."

"Until tomorrow morning then. We hold such games in late afternoon, and that will permit time to select judges. I can choose captains of visiting ships, so they have no interest in the outcome, if you like."

"Very well." Shadow rose, bowed stiffly and strode away.

He had accepted. But she wasn't sure she dared risk losing.

Lumle listened gravely to Shadow's account. "There's no shame in *mlevja,* you know," he said.

But it was not shame that disturbed her through the day and into the night; it was something else, something she had no name for. The thing that had darkened Mera's days, and led her to a futile death. The thing that made women weaken, when they lay with men, and be lessened. Argen had desired only her body. Kirji would take more, as much as he could. Even if he did not really want it.

Shadow awoke in the morning, knowing she would do whatever she must to help the people of Omaq, and Nle. She sent word to the Mage that she accepted his terms.

Chapter Eleven

The contest was held in an amphitheater on the outskirts of Ad-Kir, a wide arena with two benches for the participants to occupy while they wove their illusions. The buzz of a thousand voices filled the air, sharp with excitement. It had been a long time since anyone had dared to challenge the Mage.

In a special box sat the three judges: two men, one in a variegated robe and the other with only a cloth about his loins, and a woman dressed in animal hides, her hair twisted into cones on either side of her head.

Shadow had slept poorly, and the day had passed with painful slowness since she'd gone to the Mage that morning to agree to the contest. Her head felt heavy, her hands swollen and her mouth dry. She felt as though everyone was staring at her disdainfully. There would be no pity if she failed to entertain them, yet the clarity was no spectacle of light and fire. Still, it was not these Kirites that mattered but the actual outcome.

The crowd cheered as the Mage entered the arena. He nodded politely to Shadow, who had preceded him, and directed the audience to applaud her. It did so begrudgingly, eager to see the illusions, impatient with this unimposing challenger.

The private Kirji had become the public Mage, draped in turquoise so that his eyes shone with unusual intensity. When he moved, he gestured grandly, a halo of light dancing around him—illusory, of course. But even seen through the clarity, he sparkled with exhilaration. To him, this was a challenging game, an opportunity to stretch the mastery of his craft.

In the crowd, Shadow picked out Dorf's solid figure hulking over those around him. Plain, faithful Dorf. Seeing him, she imagined she heard the scurrying of feet as city-sneaks darted through the maze of Ad-Omaq, smelled the stink of its sewers, felt the touch of Nle's hand on her arm. The memories helped calm her nervousness.

The woman judge nodded that the hour had begun. Kirji tapped his fingers together, and a bloodcat leaped at Shadow, its keening wail shivering through the assembly. She yawned, and was rewarded by a smattering of laughter.

Clearly, the Mage did not expect to fool her so easily. He was showing off to amuse his audience, and succeeding. A family of illusion munts cavorted across Shadow's feet. A ring-babble ran out and killed one, dropping it into her hand. She ignored it.

"Whenever you're ready to begin," she said.

A ripple moved through the audience at her audacity. Kirji frowned and gazed at the sky. "I think we have picked a bad day for our contest." Overhead, dark clouds gathered, blotting out the afternoon sunlight, and birds from the sea circled and mewed as if distressed.

"Perhaps we should take cover," called one of the judges. "The storm moves in from the southeast."

"These sudden tempests are noted for their violence," the Mage explained to Shadow.

"Are they noted also for leaving sun's warmth on one's shoulders, my lord?"

The clouds vanished. Applause sounded from the audience, but she thought it was more for the Mage's ability to fool them than for her own alertness.

"Shadow!" Lumle pushed his way to the edge of the arena. "You must stop this contest. I've had a message from the Council." Shadow remained where she was, uncertain how to proceed. "Please, ask the judges for a respite."

Kirji leaned forward on his bench. "You concede defeat, if you do. Your friend attempts to trick me." An angry murmur arose from the audience at this interruption of their entertainment.

Tricks. Was the message real, or had Lumle been deceived? There were many ways the Mage might mislead her. The man sitting opposite her might even be a illusion, with the real Kirji standing invisible nearby.

Alarmed, Shadow checked with the clarity. The Mage was real enough. A sweep of the arena showed it bare of anything else, including Lumle.

"Clever of you, to send an image of my friend," she said.

A brief silence, and then the watchers understood, even as the appreciation faded. There was more clapping and a few cheers, again more for the Mage than for Shadow, although she felt the beginning of a reluctant admiration.

She must remember to use the clarity frequently, even when she suspected nothing. He had almost defeated her, so early in the contest. It was not only his illusions she must battle but his cunning, his ability to cut to the heart and distort what he found there.

Kirji regarded her with good humor, as if he would have been disappointed were the contest to end so easily. "You will, of course, wish to make the most of this opportunity. There are many things that can be shown with illusions, things that I have seen and you might wish to see."

"You tell me openly that these will be illusions?"

"Yes. But you must signal me thus"—he lifted his hand slightly—"from time to time, to show that you have not forgotten."

"Why should I agree to play the game this way?"

"How else can the daughter of Taav and Mera see Ad-Son, without leaving the Eastern Lands?"

Shadow checked with the clarity, to be sure he had not left an image of himself while the real Mage walked elsewhere in the arena, and found he had not. Even as she did so, she weighed the dangers of following his plan. Clearly, he had some purpose for proposing it, perhaps thinking she would be caught up, and so she might be.

And it was possible the illusions he wove would be lies, false pictures of Ad-Son that would distort her thinking in the future. But Lumle would see them, too, from where he sat, and tell her the truth later. It was irresistible, the chance to see and hear and smell the fabled city where the Council met. As the Mage had known it would be.

"Very well." Shadow heard the audience rustle as if settling down for an enjoyable show.

Although she had experienced the snares in the forest, Shadow was unprepared for the authenticity of the creation that closed around her now. She stood on the prow of a ship, Kirji beside her, smelling the salt breeze and the oily tang of fish as they sailed into a harbor. The lack of sensation—the ship did not roll, nor the wind chill her cheeks—gave the scene a dreamlike haze. But, like a dream, it took on its own reality.

A cliff soared straight up from the harbor, cut by a narrow curving path packed with men and an unfamiliar breed of pack animals, smaller than a harthorn but sturdier. From where she stood the path appeared to take on a life of its own. Old women sold drinks at the elbow-turns; traders hawked wares spread on blankets; and the travelers proceeded at a leisurely pace, eating, drinking and bargaining as they went.

Atop the cliff spread a plateau, vibrant with the colors of a marketplace and the surrounding state buildings. Behind it reared a second cliff, crowned by a white pillared palace. Shadow blinked, concentrated, and the scene vanished, although the audience around her stared raptly. She lifted her hand to Kirji, then returned to Ad-Son and listened to the coarse voices as she and the Mage debarked. Around them, dockworkers spoke with clicks and hisses, while others chattered in piercingly high tones. A band of women marched by, clad in leather, barking at anyone who ventured into their path.

The image of Kirji beside her turned. "Perhaps you would like to visit the marketplace and make some purchases." The wind of Ad-Son ruffled through his hair; he looked younger in this vision and lighter of heart. He must have visited Ad-Son some years ago, perhaps before taking over the rule of Kir. "There is also the temple to the Old Gods, and the Council Chambers."

As he spoke, she used the clarity again, and saw

that the Kirites remained transfixed. Again, she signaled her awareness. "The Library," Shadow said.

At this, the Mage hesitated, but only for a fraction of a moment. "You do wish to test my powers, indeed. There we will find echoes of the past, and illusions within illusions."

"But you will do it, because how better to trick me?" Even through the noise of Ad-Son, she heard whispers of appreciation run through the watchers in the amphitheater.

"Yes; the Library." The young Mage flexed his shoulders, preparing for the challenge, and they found themselves on the top of the second cliff. Below, the harbor had shrunk till it appeared scarcely bigger than the tabletop scenes in the room where she had first met Kirji.

Turning, Shadow saw that the Library was built of stone which looked white, but from close up shimmered with soft colors. Above, on the frieze, the Mage pointed out an inscription.

Oddly, Shadow found she could read it, although it seemed unlikely it was written in the language of the Eastern Lands. Had Kirji translated it for this vision, or did it translate itself?

It said, "To know what is, you first must see truly."

Reminded, Shadow gestured to Kirji. Her arm felt leaden, as if begrudging the distraction. The compulsion to enter, to delve into this storehouse of the past, was so great that Shadow considered halting the illusion altogether. But surely she could withstand a few more minutes, enough to taste what lay inside.

They walked up the steps, through double doors that stood wide. "Can anyone come here?" she asked.

"Yes, but few do, other than scholars. The climb

discourages them, and the marketplace has its own enticements."

They entered a great hall, the ceiling as high above as the mast of a ship might tower, the walls covered with bookshelves and books.

"I wish in my lifetime I could read even a tenth of them," said the Mage. "I doubt anyone has read them all. Some of the languages are lost. The Council sends expeditions to the farthest limits of our maps, hoping to rediscover forgotten lands or uncover new ones; and there are always those who sail beyond the maps, but most never come back. There are scholars, too, who work at deciphering the old tongues, but it is a slow business."

"Could you show me a page from one?" asked Shadow.

"Perhaps, if I can recall it clearly. The shape of the writing is beautiful in itself." After a moment of deep thought, Kirji lifted down a volume and opened it.

For one instant of clarity, Shadow caught an image of an old man with an elongated neck and a disease-pocked face, bent over a page by lamplight, scratching with a quill pen. He wrote of a plague, and a civilization destroyed. . . .

Then the man vanished along with the page, and she saw the amphitheater in Ad-Kir where everyone but her sat enthralled. She motioned to the Mage and returned to the dream.

Shadow described what she had seen. "If I went to Ad-Son, I might penetrate those books. Not through reading them, but through the clarity."

For the first time, real interest touched the Mage's face. In his hesitation, Shadow felt him weigh this new possibility, this unexpected facet of the clarity, and then felt him brush the perception aside, discounting it.

"Surely you would like to see some of the rooms." Kirji led her from the entrance hall into a sparsely peopled corridor from which other passageways branched. "Do you wish to see the History Room of Omaq?"

At her nod, they found themselves in another hallway. Fearing she might become too absorbed, Shadow hastily returned her attention to the arena, and so indicated.

Then they stepped through a door into another world. This was no mere room but open sky and mountains, fresh green trees and a brook rippling over flat stones. This was Omaq as it had looked when Shadow was a child. As the Mage had said, it was an illusion within an illusion.

"How is this done?" she asked.

"My father worked here and others before him, Mages of Kir and the illusion-gifted of other lands. We try to preserve civilizations and peoples, so that in future they will not be forgotten."

At her prompting, he explained that the Library had been established during the early decades of the first Council, five hundred years before. At that time, expeditions had begun to lands known and unknown. The expansion of the Library was the duty of each new generation.

Studying the vivid landscape before her, Shadow asked, "How long can illusions endure?"

"Some have been here five centuries; they begin to fade in places and must be restored. We have no illusions older than that."

Reminded, Shadow touched the reality of Ad-Kir with her mind, and signaled.

It was with pleasure that she returned to the likeness of Omaq, to the mountains where she had lived
with Mera. "In what age are we?"

"Before the establishment of the Citadel." Kirji
followed, indulgent, as Shadow strode into the landscape, finding that while it appeared to continue for
a great distance, her steps brought her quickly into
the foothills. Here the horned race had lived and
practiced its arts in a world she had believed irre-
trievably lost to her.

Ahead lay a village unlike any she had seen. Half-
tunneled into the sides of hills, the houses emerged
as demi-globes, illuminated from within. This was
clearly the work of Radiants. In those days, they had
been scattered, one or two to a village, revered for
their skills, plying the light-arts as a means to enrich
and not to enslave.

Children ran between the houses. Some bore horns,
and one had yellow eyes. A tall woman emerged
from a doorway to call in one of the children, and
Shadow understood her words, for the language had
changed little in its isolation. She watched a time
longer, hoping to see or hear some clue to the origins of the clarity, but this was only an image, static,
unable to pierce beyond the knowledge of those who
had created it.

How much had they known, those Mages who had
shaped this likeness centuries ago? Gesturing to prove
she was not fooled, Shadow asked Kirji to show her
one of the caves.

"You seek the grayvers?" he asked. "To what end?"

"You have never entered a cave here before?"

"There was no need of it." But he ceased his
questioning, and in an instant they faced a crevice in
the rocks. The village was far behind them now,

down a valley and almost out of sight. The subtle variations within the illusion, and within Kirji's re-creation of it, went beyond anything Shadow had expected. What other uses might there be, what benefits to the people, what untapped beauty in this gift of the Mage's that he had turned instead to creating death-traps in the forest?

Shadow crouched and lowered herself into the cavern, dropping a short way onto a stone floor hollowed by the rains and softened by leaves and grasses. From the back of the cave came an eerie pale glow, a whiteness that distended itself, advancing toward her until she felt its cold glare on her face like a searchlight.

He was there, the Graylord, and in that moment he became aware of her. He reached out for her, trying to speak in her mind, in the small gray patch that belonged to him. *Together. All of us together, in Ad-Omaq. You and Briala, duality and oneness, joining with me. In three we are made whole.*

He was real, unquestionably real, but he had reached her through . . . What was it? Illusion. Yes, of course, the cave was an illusion. It wasn't real; nor the mountains, nor the vision of Omaq; they were in the Library at Ad-Son. No! Not in the Library at all; in . . .

The clarity wouldn't come, not at first, in the confusion of sight upon sight. And then she caught a faint outline . . . circling tiers of seats . . . and then the arena, and Kirji sitting there smiling.

Shadow lifted her hand. Was she in time? She sank back wearily on her bench, exhausted by the effort of wrenching free and the shock of the Graylord's intrusion.

"You did better than I expected," said the Mage.

The woman judge stood up. "The hour is over. The last bout was very close, but it is our decision that Mera-ti has won." The audience applauded quietly, still half-enraptured by the vision of Ad-Son. Kirji bowed to Shadow, with no appearance of regret.

In the amphitheater, Lumle and Dorf waited for Shadow, but Kirji halted her. "Before you celebrate with your friends, perhaps you will come with me. We need to draw up the documents that bind me to your service, as we agreed."

She would have told him how nearly overwhelmed she had been, and how his illusions lingered within her, as real as experience. But the Mage of Kir required no praise. From the line of his jaw and the mysterious smile playing about his mouth, it was clear this defeat meant nothing to him. Only a game. And so he still believed the clarity was a trick, nothing more. He would never admit, even now, that Shadow's skill was ancient, or perhaps ordained, and vital to her people.

They entered the palace by a side gate. Passing the illusion-garden, they came to his residence. Kirji ordered food and drink, and a servant nodded and withdrew as the Mage led the way into his private quarters.

They stepped into a round lounging-room bathed in rich late-afternoon light shining through a glass dome. In the center of the room, steam drifted from a small pool circled by velvet couches.

Kirji pulled a cord and a translucent blue curtain whispered into place. They stood in a private world of water and sunlight. Shadow sank onto one of the couches, inhaling the perfumed steam of the pool, as Kirji withdrew paper and pen from a small desk.

Weariness made her drowsy, as if she really had

journeyed to Ad-Son. Well, the contact with the Graylord had been real enough.

"Had I won, we would be enjoying this pool," the Mage said as he dipped the pen in an inkwell, and the thought of hot water brought twinges to Shadow's stiff muscles. "But now we must draft our agreement."

"The invisibility for me and Dorf; can you disguise our scent and sounds as well?"

"A small matter." He wrote it down. "I can arrange your safe passage through the forest and your invisibility when you arrive, but beyond that I may not interfere with events at Ad-Omaq. You understand that I may not offer any further help?"

Shadow wondered why the servant was taking so long bringing refreshments. "Of course."

"What will you do, once your task is accomplished?" The Mage leaned back. "What is this friend to you?"

"Nle? Like a brother."

"No more?"

"No."

"I know little of the customs in Ad-Omaq," the Mage confessed. Shadow wondered that he would talk so freely with her; but in some ways they had come to know each other through the contest. "Odd, isn't it, that I have visited Ad-Son and Kirrillea but not my own neighbor. The countries are very different."

"More than one who has not been there can imagine." The perfume from the pool percolated through Shadow's blood and she stretched languorously.

"You have no Symmetry of Six, I believe. How then does a man take a woman as his lover?"

"Usually by force. Unless she is Highborn, or a peasant in the countryside; then they may marry. And some of the Radiants keep concubines."

"And—no. I have no right to ask such questions."
Kirji blotted the ink on the paper.

An unfamiliar mood had come over Shadow—lazy,
comfortable, unafraid. "What is it?"

"Whether you had a lover in Ad-Omaq."

She thought back to the Den of Ashi, and Argen.
"Almost, once. But I escaped."

To her astonishment, the Mage burst forth with a
laugh. "Escaped? So this is your opinion of men!
Although I shouldn't wonder at it, if matters are as
savage in Ad-Omaq as you draw them. It was not my
intention, in offering you *mlevja*, to harm or degrade
you."

"I think you wanted to test the clarity more than
anything else," she said. "Although you would have
taken my body as well."

"These matters are more complex than you realize." The Mage moved from his desk to sit beside
her. "There would have been no coercion. Today, I
would have invited you to float with me in the water,
and you would feel it caress your skin. We would eat
our meal alone here, and then sleep wrapped in furs.
Each day that you stayed with me, you would make
new discoveries within yourself. Your body would
become a stranger to you and then a new friend, so
sensitive the murmur of my breath on your neck
would arouse desire. And one night, when we
emerged from the pool, you would pull me down
beside you, and then I would teach you what a man
can be to a woman."

Shadow felt as if he were stroking her, although
they did not touch.

"Will you join me, of your own free will?" asked
the Mage. "There is such a relationship, *shohaja*,
which lasts only as long as both partners wish it."

"Yes, perhaps." A sigh. How very, very tired she was. "Let me sign the paper and we will be done with that." She reached to take the document from his hand. It wasn't there.

Confused, Shadow groped again. And felt nothing. No paper, and no hand.

With the slight strength that remained, she dispelled the room and the pool. She was still in the arena and Kirji was sitting opposite her, smiling.

This time she knew why.

Chapter Twelve

The contest would be long remembered among the residents of Kir and those foreigners fortunate enough to have been there. Filing from the amphitheater, they spoke of it in hushed tones as though it were already a legend.

"No one could have done better," Lumle said as Shadow stood with her friends, stunned by her defeat. "I just heard one of the judges say he believed, at the end, that he was actually watching you and Kirji return to the palace."

"You did your best." Only the tightness of Dorf's voice revealed his own despondency, that this last chance for Nle had been lost.

Across the arena, Kirji stood, politely acknowledging congratulations. Shadow said good-bye to her friends as if she were leaving on a long journey, but she did not tell them her thoughts.

Anyone raised in the mire of Ad-Omaq knew that even the most tightly guarded caravan offered pickings to the quick and the sly. The Mage of Kir was rich beyond measure, not only in possessions but in skills and knowledge, tricks and power. Tightly guarded, indeed, but perhaps not invulnerable to one who would spend a week with him, an intimate week.

Shadow crossed to the wizard, her expression impassive. "Are there papers to sign?"

"No. *Mlevja* is well defined in our custom." He turned away from Vank, who had been among the first to honor his lord. "Let us have something to drink."

They walked together to his quarters in the palace. The route was familiar, as in the illusion. Even the light was the same through the glass dome, and the soothing steam from the water, and the fragrance brushing across Shadow's skin like a feather.

Sipping from a vial of bittersweet drink, she watched the Mage. His eyes looked darker than they had in sunlight, more contemplative but also more restless. Perhaps the contest had tired him, too.

"The customs of *mlevja* are not known to me." She set her drink aside. "Shall I bring you dinner?"

He leaned forward, gazing at her as one would look into a fire. "A *mlevja* mate is not a serving girl. Rather, I should bring your food."

"Why?"

"To soften your mood, which is as dark as your hair, although you try to restrain it." He reached out and smoothed a strand that had fallen across her cheek. Pushing it back, his finger brushed one of her horns.

She would not say that, of course, her mood was dark, that the loss of the contest meant the death of a friend and perhaps of Omaq itself; such railings would do nothing but amuse this man, or perhaps annoy him. And he must be soothed—not won, for she considered that impossible, but lulled. "It's just that I'm inexperienced in these matters."

The Mage drew his hand away. "You seemed willing to join in *shohaja*, when I asked you in the illusion."

"It would have been the same. My—discomfort—is that of ignorance. I trust you will help me cure it."

His turquoise eyes widened a fraction. "You speak boldly."

"Is that not proper for a woman in Ad-Kir? I can be more modest, if you like." Shadow wondered how much of her purpose was evident to the Mage and feared he found her as transparent as the dome above them, through which filtered the last rays of sunset.

Of his own thoughts, he gave no sign. "You must be as you are. Let us go together and eat."

They dined in near-silence, aware of the curious looks of the others in the courtyard. Covertly, Shadow studied the Highborn women. She had never regarded such creatures before except to see how she might steal from them. There was a womanliness to their movements as they raised a glass, a delicate self-awareness in the turn of a head, the lift of an eyebrow. She could not mimic these without awkwardness, she admitted silently. Her own direct manner was all she had, unsuitable as it might be.

Yet when they returned to the Mage's quarters, she saw that he was far away in his mind, and doubted any coquetry would have beguiled him. Wrapped in a fur robe, Shadow watched the play of emotions across his high-boned face. Perhaps he thought of the Council. A message-bird had arrived that morning to say that Fia and the Lord Chamberlain were returning. It did not, according to Lumle, reveal what the Council had decided. For such important news, a bird was too frail a messenger.

At last the Mage regarded her. "Make use of the pool, if you wish." He spoke indifferently, as if he did not care whether she stayed or went.

How would it be, to touch him with the clarity, to reach inside him? It might be possible, but it would surely anger him. And through the channel that was opened, he in turn might see into her heart, and might take away more than he lost.

Lying warm in her fur, Shadow let her eyes close. She had meant to find some way to become his lover tonight, but she had not the art for it. When she slept, it was too deeply to dream.

She awoke alone, finding fresh clothing, food and towels by the pool. Grateful for the solitude, she slid into the heated water. She floated in it as long as she dared, hoping the Mage would return, and that the perfume and steam might work on him as they had on her. But after a time, growing restless, she emerged and dried herself.

A short while later, as if servants had been watching, Kirji came in. "Would you care to see more of Ad-Kir?" His manner was pleasant but impersonal. As he spoke, he buckled on a knife-belt, no doubt taking her consent for granted. And, indeed, Shadow had no intention of refusing.

They left the confining walls of the palace and passed through the noisy marketplace. Shadow began to feel more like herself—watchful, ready to fight if need be, although she had no knife. She was momentarily surprised that the Mage dared walk unguarded through the city, but then she realized that he had his weapon, and, more important, he could summon an army of illusions with the turn of a thought.

They watched three veiled women uncoil a sensuous dance upon a ruby carpet. "Are they from Kirrillea?" she asked.

"The Mystic Scent Dancers?" The Mage chuckled. "No, only traveling entertainers. You can find their like in any bazaar in the Council lands."

They left the marketplace and walked along a broad street lined with shops, open at the front to display their wares. Instinctively, Shadow assessed the lack of guards and stretched her shoulders to measure the the space left within her pack, then remembered she carried none that day.

Her movement had not escaped the Mage's notice. At his questioning look, Shadow said, "Your city would be easy pickings for a thief."

"Your clarity, as you call it, may be a useful tool, but you are still less than expert in its use."

Then she saw what she had not thought to look for: Enforcers protected by invisibility, patrolling the thoroughfare.

So the Mage believed her unskilled. Perhaps he was right; Shadow didn't yet know the reaches of her clarity. But it troubled her that he regarded her gift so lightly.

He drew her attention by gesturing at a shop that displayed works of glass and metal, lamps and navigational aids, necklaces that glowed with their own light and shimmering strands to weave through the hair. They had been made, he said, by the handful of Radiants who had fled Omaq years ago.

"Much might be accomplished, more than has yet been conceived, if Ad-Omaq would rejoin the Council," he said.

"Not under Briala. My lord—"

"There is much prejudice between you and your

sister. You cannot help but think ill of her; in your place, I would, also." He turned away to show her the temple as they passed it, a domed structure of blue stone with a frieze carved of strange symbols and unfamiliar animals. There, the Mage said, visitors to Kir might worship their own idols, and Kirites pray to the sea-god Ahrenki, and unbelievers leave an offering to any watching gods, in case they did exist after all.

When they had gone beyond the temple, Shadow spoke again, hurrying to get the words out before Kirji could stop her. "I heard Briala speak to Hakin when I was seeking my friend within the Citadel. It made no sense, that she would rather face the grayvers than seek a treaty with Kir, but that's what she said. And then Hakin died suddenly, only a few days later . . ." In her haste, Shadow knew she had failed to explain clearly. "My lord, I think the grayvers must have given Hakin something of value, something Briala wanted terribly."

"From a fragment of a conversation? Easily misunderstood."

A deep breath enabled Shadow to hold back her sharp reply. Whatever she said to Kirji, it would not persuade him, and it might turn him against her.

They left the avenue for winding side streets that led toward the water. "You've seen something of our games," the Mage said. "Let me show you how the common people play them."

In this sector of the city, Shadow observed few women, and the men were scarred and painted with crude symbols. Two boys pushed by, horns spiraling down from the crowns of their heads. The Mage slid his knife from its sheath with less than a sliver of sound. The horns quivered and, daggers ready, the boys whirled and she saw that they were actually grown men, small but hard.

"I beg your pardon." The Mage showed them his hands, empty. "I made a demonstration for this woman, who is of the old race of Omaq and has never seen the old race of Son before."

The men glared suspiciously, and then one recognized the Mage. They nodded almost imperceptibly and moved on.

The street descended and narrowed. Mingling with the scents of brine and fish were the effervescence of finot and the heavier, bittersweet smell of strong drink. A band of sailors spilled out of a doorway, cursing in a foreign tongue. "In here." Kirji let Shadow enter first.

Chairs and tables had been cleared back. A dozen men and a bald, heavyset woman crouched in a circle around two bands of tiny illusion-warriors, each about the height of a finger, the work, no doubt, of Kirite artisans. The woman shouted orders to one troop; a one-legged man commanded the other. The miniature fighters chopped and slashed, hacking off limbs and heads. The wounded twisted and screamed as they fell, then vanished.

"Cleverly made," Shadow murmured.

"Barkeep!" The bald woman tossed some coins. "A Radiant!"

An angry murmur arose from her opponent, who was forced to buy his own Radiant. The two hooded figures joined the battle, searing each other and the troops until the figures blackened in hideous torment. At least, only one figure was left—not a Radiant, but a young soldier. The woman cursed, and money was exchanged.

"A tedious business, I should think, if they play it often," Shadow said when they reached the street again.

"Oh, the wealthy play more elaborate games." The Mage guided her along the waterfront, where great ships dwarfed the docks; some bore insignia on their sails, and other defiant colors, scarlet and black, amber and jade. "Sometimes there are hundreds of life-size combatants; armies of Radiants."

"And you take pleasure in this?"

"In war? Never. In the semblance of it? I see no harm; it's a useful diversion, for there are many races of people in Ad-Kir, and they need a safe outlet for their aggressions."

A low whistle caught Shadow's ear, and she turned to see a woman lounging in a doorway, summoning a sailor, who stopped to bargain with her. Here and there along the wharves, she saw others, like those in the Street of Lost Women, posing their bodies to sell to men. But they were not chained.

"So you have this even in Ad-Kir." She didn't try to hide her distaste. "I was told the Symmetry of Six involved no degradation."

"There is no shame in *slevjak*."

"No shame? In that?"

Kirji's mouth tightened as he followed her gaze. "We are not always one with our ideals."

He could stop it, if he wished. Yet clearly he disapproved. Shadow's confusion must have shown, for he added, "My people may obtain training in any skill without charge, if they are willing to work hard. But there will always be those who prefer the easy life."

"Easy?"

"At first it may seem so." They passed an alleyway where a man and woman lay sprawled amid the refuse, sharing a smoking-rod from which Shadow caught a sickly sweetish odor. "There are no restrictions in Ad-Kir on anything one does privately. In places, the air becomes so full of vapors, one's mind clouds walking through."

She made no objection when they turned onto a road that led upward, away from the harbor. "I should think illusions would be enough."

"For some people, nothing but death is enough." For the first time, the Mage's voice betrayed his anger. "Waste. Cursed waste, all of it. Do you know what we could do if the Eastern Lands were united in peace? Come this way. I think it will help you understand me." He strode ahead so rapidly she had to quicken her pace.

A short distance later they turned at a gate and passed up a few steps and into a large, light-washed building. Shadow had an impression of rooms spinning off corridors on either side of them, of quiet, blue-clad figures moving along the hallways. The air smelled medicinal, like the plants Mera had dried and ground for her ointments.

In an antechamber, through a clear pane, they watched two women and a man bend over a young girl. One of the women lifted a knife and drew it across the top of the girl's head, so that blood welled up. Shadow's eyes burned; she remembered the boy, ripped open by ghouls in the foothills of Omaq. "Why? How can you allow this?"

The Mage read from a panel above the glass. "She has a growth in the brain. Already her vision is affected, and she will die without the operation."

"But the pain—"

"There is none." He indicated one of the women. "She creates illusions in the mind, not visible to the others, for whom they would be a distraction. The child believes herself to be in some safe, cheerful place, perhaps playing with a ring-babble. We find that the mind can close out pain."

There was no pretense in his passion. Shadow's distrust of the Mage softened; he was a man who cared for his people, as she wished Taav had done.

He went on: "We have performed experiments with the narrow-light, but our Radiants are few. If Ad-Omaq were to join us, we could rid ourselves of much suffering. Perhaps someday we would even find the secret to strengthening the souls that you witnessed at the waterfront. Who knows what might be accomplished?"

Her steps matched his as they left the building and ascended toward the palace. His anger at the waste of lives drew them closer. Had he not been the Mage, he would still have been extraordinary.

They were apart the rest of the day, he with his business, Shadow with Lumle and Dorf. She told what she had seen, but not all the Mage had said. She felt uncertain how much to reveal, as if she owed a loyalty to Kirji even above that to her friends.

In the evening, he returned late from meetings with his councillors. The ship had not come, was not expected for several days, but they wished to be prepared for whatever the Council might have decided. The possibility of Ad-Omaq rejecting a treaty was not taken seriously. Instead, the Mage told her, he was ordering blast-powder to be stockpiled so it might be put at Briala's disposal, for use against the grayvers.

"May I travel with you if you go to Ad-Omaq?"

She lay wrapped in fur, watching firelight touch his weary eyes.

"If it does not violate the Council's directive or your sister's wishes. But would you wish to go if, as you say, the grayvers march against the city?"

"Even so."

"You haven't spoken of it, but I think you want to rule Omaq as your father did before you. Is that not true?" The question hung darkly in the air, a threat to all Shadow's plans.

She answered carefully. "I seek, as you do, to see my people free, safe and at peace. If I must lead to accomplish that, then, yes, I would."

"But if your sister can achieve these goals?"

For the past dozen years, the knowledge of Shadow's heritage and the prospect of someday seizing it had fueled her dreams. More than that, it had given her a reason to keep struggling at times when the viciousness of life within Ad-Omaq nearly overwhelmed her. But if she had to give it up, for the good of her land, surely she would find the strength. "I'm not ambitious for myself, my lord. If I must step aside, I will."

The Mage made no further comment. Again that night, they slept apart, but Shadow was aware of him dozing restlessly nearby.

On the third day, she awoke to strange music, a humming in her blood. The Mage's chambers had vanished, giving way to an alien landscape of green, all green, trees drooping with moss, an encampment of green pavilions, green steam bubbling up from pots set into firepits. The air was thick with rich steam-scents, each bringing a memory of a place never seen, an emotion never before experienced, a season hitherto unknown on the earth.

Perceiving it to be illusion, and guessing it to be Kirrillea, Shadow inhaled the perfume and marveled at the Mage's genius. Again came the music, and with it blue and green bubbles floated up from the pots, forming vague figures in the air that slowly took on shape and dimension and became dancers. Men and women with glowing bodies, soft swelling muscles, sensuous hips and shoulders undulated around Shadow. Half-turning, she saw Kirji reclining nearby, a youthful mischief in his smile.

The dancers surrounded them, touched them, became them. In a green glow, Shadow found her body a voluptuous thing that belonged to the music, to the Mage, and he to her. Skin dazzled against skin, and fragrance enveloped them, the scent of their own longing mingling in the opulence of Kirrillea, in the steam of the pool, the Mage's pool. They had joined in one realm and been transported to another, back to Ad-Kir, where they lay tangled in furs, their bodies now less than two but more than one.

He drew her gently against him, his mouth upon hers, and then tenderness deepened so that nothing existed, only her arms tightening about his neck and his arms clasping her. No further illusions were necessary.

The closeness that grew between Shadow and the Mage in the next days was mistrusted by them both and yet strengthened with each hour together. She could touch his mind with the clarity, when he was drowsy and open to her, and found there a vulnerability that surprised her.

He would forget his formal ways with her, relaxing into honesty. She listened to tales of old Kir, of the days before the separation of Omaq, and he told of

his father, who had died bitter that the Eastern
Lands had become not closer but more remote with
each passing year.

In turn, Kirji asked of Mera, and the ways of the
city, and the grayvers. Shadow felt him sifting the
information, weighing it on the scale of his own
purposes. It was difficult not to press him, not to
insist that he assess the strengths and weaknesses of
the clarity and the Graylord and the Radiants as she
did. But she taught herself patience, hour by hour.

And often she had no need of it. For there was
more to their time together than words or tales. In
Kirji's warmth, Shadow discovered a flowering in
herself, as if a seed had lain untended and only now
found sunlight and water. Wondering at this velvet
unfolding, she came to know more of her mother's
love for Taav. The anger that had lived in Shadow
since Mera pushed her away in the crowd at Ad-
Omaq, that had been tempered but not destroyed by
adult understanding, faded at last, and she saw the
world in a new way.

Yet still, at night, when she gazed up at the sky,
the three moons seemed to hover close to earth. The
two smaller ones clung to the glow of the third,
which scanned Kir like a giant eye. When she slept,
she saw Migal's people struggling against the ghouls
on a black field; or Taav, walking away from Mera
with a careless wave; or Ashi in his Den, holding out
a glass that might contain finot, or aka-poison.

The future waited on a white sail, carrying word of
the Council's ruling. When, at the end of a week,
Silla raced into the garden to tell them the ship had
been sighted, Shadow followed Kirji to greet his
sister with the same apprehension as when she had

lifted Ashi's cup to her lips, not knowing what it
held.

The news was this: Briala had agreed to a treaty
with Kir against the grayvers in return for a store of
blast-powder. To ensure peace, she proposed a marriage of state—*regaja*—between herself and the Mage.

And so it was to be. The Council had ordered it.

Chapter Thirteen

The first time Briala heard the voice, she thought it was Kah-geb. Coming out of a dream, she couldn't fully understand the words; something about the time being near.

She muttered and rolled over in the silken sheets, reaching for her cousin. No one was there.

Briala's eyes flew open and her muscles tensed. Attack. She'd been expecting one at any moment for weeks now. One couldn't stay awake forever. But if Kah-geb had turned against her, whom could she trust?

When nothing moved in the room, she eased herself up into a sitting position. The chamber was large but, at her instruction, without wall hangings or long curtains that might hide an enemy. Still, Briala studied the room for any hint of danger.

A large window gave over the city and the barren countryside beyond, its glass mirrored on the outside to maintain privacy. Everything in the room she had made herself, so as to know its secrets: the glass lamps, the wood furniture, even the bricks in the fireplace. All but the clothes. She could not sew with a beam of light.

Satisfied at last that there was no one else present, she dismissed the voice as a figment of her dream. It had been the old nightmare, the one about Taav, which now alternated with the new one about Hakin. At least I get a bit of variety, Briala reflected ironically, stepping naked from the bed to become a trio of elfin women in the adjacent triptych of mirrors.

She still hadn't quite become accustomed to the new luster of her body, Briala reflected as she shrugged into a long velvet gown. Neither her clear skin nor the golden hue of her eyes gave any sign of the debauches in which she had indulged since Hakin's death. Although she did feel a little tired this morning.

Briala treated herself to one of her enchanting smiles as she ran a silver brush through her dark hair. Even she wasn't immune to the allure lent by the gift. And with men, if she cared to exert herself, she had discovered she could work a magic that overcame the most profound aversion.

"Cousin?" After a quick rap at the door, Kah-geb entered. He had chosen a robe of bronze silk today, one that made no attempt to hide the incongruities of his body. The masculine bulge below the belted waist was delineated no less clearly than the swell of breasts above. Once compelled to slink about in the back ways of the Citadel, the Highborn hermaphrodite reveled in his rise to power since Briala's accession.

"Yes?" She fixed him with a stern eye. Had he been in her bed last night? She couldn't remember, now. It didn't matter.

"A Council messenger has arrived from Kir." His narrow eyes regarded her questioningly.

"Send the man to my sitting room. It is a man?"

Briala smoothed down the front of her gown. A hold-over from earlier times. Preening was no longer necessary.

"Yes. A squat sort of fellow—"

"Well? Don't just stand there. Bring him in!"

Kah-geb bowed, his lips curving as if amused by her childish display of temper, and retreated. The man—thing—was becoming almost insolent at times, as if he fancied himself her equal. He was a useful tool, but like a bloodcat he might someday turn on his master.

Briala passed through another door, this one leading to the ornate sitting room, also decorated by her own hand. She chose a seat by the window. Men always underestimated a woman who was sitting down.

The visitor entered, a short man who said his name was Lumle. She had seen him before, she realized, as he delivered the required civilities. "You must be the one who left the message-bird without our noticing. I saw you emptying the slop pots that day. You are dedicated, indeed."

His face creased in a polite smile. "The Council demands a great deal from its servants." His gaze fixed on her face, not in fascination but curiosity. As if he were comparing her to someone.

There could be only one woman in the world who looked like Briala. Was it possible her half-sister had survived her leap into the river? Had Mera-ti gone to the Council demanding to be instated as ruler of Omaq?

The messenger was speaking again. "I come to report that the Mage of Kir accepts your peace offer. He and a small party will arrive here in one week's time for the ceremony of *regaja*."

"And the blast-powder?"

"He will bring it."

Briala traced one finger down the line of her cleavage, uncaring what the messenger might think. What would it be like, making love with a sorcerer? "I'm pleased to see you avoided the ghouls outside our walls. You didn't arrive on wings, perchance?"

"The Mage contrived to protect me."

As if she needed reminding that her future husband was not to be lightly dismissed! But clearly this envoy would reveal nothing willingly, apart from his official message. Still, he might be manipulated to her ends. "If you should encounter Mera-ti—"

"Mera-ti?"

"My half-sister. Perhaps she is in Kir?" He didn't respond. Well, if Mera-ti indeed survived, the bastard must be lured back, and this messenger was Briala's only means of accomplishing that. "Naturally, she will be welcome here. In honor of the treaty, Omaq lifts its ban on the old race. And she may come to live in the Citadel. I'll see that she's gowned and jeweled as befits the daughter of Taav." There, that should tempt the little bitch.

"On behalf of the Council, I applaud your graciousness." Was that irony in his tone?

His indifference to her troubled Briala. Since Hakin's death, men had generally succumbed to the Radiant's beauty even without any attempt to lure them. Was it possible that Mera-ti resembled Briala closely enough to inure men to her?

Briala waited one more moment, in case the messenger might add anything, then stood. "Do you stay long in my city?"

"My ship will anchor offshore tomorrow night. I've been away from home long enough."

"A safe voyage, then."

"I wish you happiness. You and your future husband." He turned and left without so much as a wistful glance back at her.

Irritated, Briala stroked a long, pointed fingernail across the back of one hand. Nasty little man; just the sort to befriend Mera-ti and scheme on her behalf, no doubt. But what harm could he do?

Her thoughts turned to the Mage. Her future husband. A powerful man; how powerful she didn't yet know. Until she did, he would find a wife who seemed as sweet in temperament as in appearance. Her full charm would bear upon him, and if he had ever seen Mera-ti, he would forget her instantly.

Nothing must be allowed to interfere until first the grayvers were mastered and then the Kirites, and Briala stood as undisputed ruler of the Eastern Lands. Mera-ti would be easily disposed of then.

But in the meantime, there was a way to twist a knife into that bastard wench's heart. As soon as Kah-geb returned, Briala said, "Bring me the prisoner Nle."

"You have other duties. The bloodcats are hungry." He made no apology for thwarting her.

"Oh, very well." She swept past her cousin and down the corridor, descending by a staircase to the less exalted levels of the Citadel. At each floor she must traverse a short passage to the next set of stairs, and everywhere eyes followed her. Some voices called greetings, which she answered with a nod.

The Radiants' lounges on the floor below her own were empty at this hour. Next Briala passed the workshops where Radiant artisans, aided by novices and Highborns, created masterpieces of glass and metal. The warehouses were full of such items already, she knew, but they would soon become a source of wealth again. Among other things her marriage would accomplish was a lifting of the trade ban.

More important by far was the school on the ground level. It looked innocent enough, merely a few chairs, tables covered by oddments of twisted metal, and the whole surrounded by wall coverings that resisted heat. The official explanation, to the Mage, would be that the novices came here to learn their skills as Radiants. And that was true, as far as it went.

But matters changed in the evenings, after the slaves retired to the lower levels, the Radiants to the upper ones, and most of the Highborns to their own houses in the city. Then a handful of adepts, under Briala's direction, refined the use of the light-powers as weapons.

The red-light was Briala's own discovery. It permitted one to see at night, without alerting one's enemy to the intrusion. So far, objects still appeared blurry, but she and her cohorts were improving it rapidly. Used with the narrow-light, it should permit the destruction of marauding ghouls and anything else that sought cover of darkness.

The key problem was to obtain enough blast-powder to destroy the grayvers, Briala reflected as she passed the floor given to weavers, potters, and other ordinary craftsmen. How ironic that she had been so opposed, when Hakin originally suggested it. But Hakin had meant to destroy the gift as well, because it had been provided her by the grayvers. Yet it was not they who had given it to Briala. The gift had come to her of its own devising upon Hakin's death, and she owed no debts for it.

Descending to the underground gardens, Briala

left the stairwell and navigated a tiled path, ignoring the sweating bodies that labored among rows of artificially lit crops. Striding past the pens of harthorns and harkbirds, she flexed her fists in annoyance. Even the powder would be difficult to use; it had to be implanted in the caves, and how was that to be done?

Curse the grayvers, whatever they were. Even Hakin hadn't found out when she visited their stronghold after Taav's death, to deal with the Graylord for the gift. Things of mist, but not invulnerable. Almost human, Hakin had said. Greedy, certainly, and Briala was well aware that their power had magnified itself since the tribute began. Then, in the past week, more and more ghouls had been spotted near the city, as well as some strange lurching figures unlike any seen before. But these could be easily picked off with the light-weapons, once the grayvers themselves were destroyed.

She crossed behind the barns and stopped, staring into the bloodcat pit. The beasts paced restlessly, snarling up at her. They were shielded from workers and anyone else who might pass by, ostensibly to protect the beasts' hypersensitive ears and noses from outside stimuli.

The slaves knew better, not the whole truth but enough to keep them terrified. Good. The mere presence of the cats made force almost unnecessary to secure obedience.

But they bred too slowly. Now that one female had been killed, there remained only a single breeding pair, plus one adult male and three kittens too young to train. More might be found beyond the mountains, so legend said, but that was out of the question for now.

Briala climbed down the ladder into the pit. Her mastery must be renewed each day, or the things would quickly turn wild.

The animals were hungry, and one stalked toward her, head lowered and tail twitching. She stung it with a touch of fire-light and it leaped back, teeth bared. Hakin had preferred to coddle them, but Briala knew her mother had carried a deep scar across her thigh, from not blasting when she should have.

The frightened keeper cringed out of his shed as she ascended from the pit. "Well?" she demanded. "Why haven't you brought the meat?"

"They're in my h-hut. S-sitting down. I'll fetch them."

Briala waited, annoyed by the delay. Finally he returned with three slaves too emaciated to be of any further use. A rough jerk of her head signaled the keeper to retreat. He hesitated, as if debating whether to speak, then fled before her glare.

"Please, Miss." The dry, cracked voice emerged from an equally dry, cracked face, recognizable as a woman only from the tattered scarf drawn around her sparse hair. "You can't really mean to do this. You're so lovely."

Briala caught the gaze of watery blue eyes with her yellow ones, transfixing the crone. The woman offered no real struggle as her soul parted from the useless body and flowed into Briala's cells. It was not a great prize, but already she could feel herself strengthening, and the slight weariness left by last night's carousing dissipated like dew in sunlight.

She released the meat, and it staggered back, face blank. An old man came next; he didn't even attempt to fight, nor did he nourish her much. And then came a child, sickly and lame, whimpering as she sucked its essence.

A shove toward the ladder and each descended blindly, unprotesting as the bloodcats slashed them to the ground. Briala wondered if that meager flesh offered the animals any more sustenance than those thin souls had given her.

She was still hungry.

The keeper hadn't emerged from his shack. He had been well warned that the price of observing this ceremony was to become next in line for it himself.

No one must know. Even Kah-geb only suspected what it was the Graylord had given Hakin and Hakin had unintentionally passed on to her daughter. They might not understand, might even be repulsed by the discovery that she, the leader of the Radiants, took souls and fed the ghoul-bodies to the bloodcats.

Or they might try to steal it from her, the secret of drawing souls that gave eternal youth and surpassing beauty, and with it power over others. But how could they steal it? She wasn't even sure how she had taken it herself.

The bloodcats were still feeding, growling distractedly as was their habit. Briala lowered herself into the pit, ready to scorch any that approached her, but the meal had sated them.

She had been curious for a long time. And what better target than the extra male, which might create trouble if it chose to fight for the female. Briala focused on the beast. Aware of her attention, it swung its head toward her. Now for the challenge: Those ruby eyes were blind.

She focused. The animal grunted and lifted its muzzle, sniffing the air and stirring uneasily. It moved

closer. She stood her ground, compelling the creature to yield up its spirit.

The air between them turned cloudy, milky-white
as Briala drew out the beast's blindness, and then
the scarlet fire of its soul. It seared the air between
them, dangerous to take.

Leave it.

That voice! Hearing it, Briala momentarily lost her
concentration, and the soul funneled back into the
bloodcat, which shook its head, dazed.

Where? She whipped around. No one was there,
and she heard no sound of anyone fleeing. The voice
had come from inside her head. Briala snatched at a
memory. Hakin—what had she said? Something about
hearing a voice and fearing it was Taav, come back
from the dead.

Nonsense. It must have been some hidden part of
Briala herself speaking. Or of the gift. It had instructed her in its own use, by instinct, and now it
was apparently continuing to do so in a more direct
manner.

The gift had come to her of its own will, and it was
her closest friend. With its aid, she had stepped
easily into Hakin's role as leader of the Radiants,
more powerful even than her mother had been since
she owed nothing to the grayvers. One of Briala's
first acts had been to cut off the tribute, since their
souls only added to the grayvers' strength. Well,
once she received the blast-powder from Kir, she
would see the last of the cursed Gray Ones.

At least she could sate her hunger with a human
soul, and spite Mera-ti at the same time. Briala
turned her steps toward the trapdoor that led to the
dungeon. Before she reached it, however, Kah-geb
appeared.

"Have you forgotten? The adepts await word from you on the message from the Council."

Duty. Briala's lip curled with distaste at the thought of the meeting. There was opposition from among the adepts, led by the Radiant Yenat, who had long sought open war against the grayvers and peace with the Council. He must be silenced before the Mage arrived.

The adepts waited in their private lounge, open only to those Radiants skilled or clever enough to win a place in the inner circle. Even they knew nothing of the message she had sent, only that a messenger from the Council had arrived here that morning to see Briala.

She stepped from the quiet dimness of the corridor through a thick door. The brightly lit room was of a good size, circular, with a round, elevated center and thick scarlet rugs woven from the wool of harthorn lambs. The Radiants, some twenty of them, sat upon low white couches. These were leaders, even among their own kind.

Here, in the evenings, they brought their concubines and slaves, drinking finot as Highborn musicians played in the elevated center. But the mood now was somber. Even as she greeted individual allies among the Radiants, Briala studied Yenat surreptitiously.

An older man, near fifty and still handsome, he had quarreled often with Briala, and with Hakin before her death. After it, he had sworn loyalty to the new leader, but there remained a space between them, a space tinged with mistrust and widened by his criticism of her inaction.

He reclined on a couch at the far side of the musicians' platform with his concubine Alea, a pretty girl with long russet hair. The daughter of a merchant impoverished by the trade ban, she held her union with Yenat to be akin to a marriage. And so, it appeared, did he.

Under ordinary circumstances, Briala would have dismissed the girl from her mind. But several times she had caught sly glances from Alea, who then quickly looked away. Was she plotting something with Yenat? If the bastard Mera-ti were to come to the Citadel and they were to take her into their plot, such an alliance could prove dangerous indeed. Briala must find a way to cut off this peril at its roots. And in the meantime, Alea must be kept in her place.

"This creature has no business here," Briala commanded.

The girl's lips paled, but she arose, made a short bow and strode out the door. "She was only waiting until you arrived, my lady," said Yenat.

Briala fought back the urge to snap at him. She must not seem to make too much of this matter.

There was already some grumbling among the Radiants, she perceived, and saw that it centered upon her own chamberlain. At her command, he came forth reluctantly to report that more ghouls had been seen. A peasant newly arrived in the city, and immediately enslaved, had sworn some of the creatures were not ghouls but corpses, stinking of decomposure.

Other adepts spoke up: Clearly the Graylord meant to launch some foul attack. Fear was affecting even the common people of the city; two attacks on Enforcers had been reported in the past week. In addition, a mob had murdered and burned one of the Lost Women as a sacrifice, apparently believing ancient tales that the grayvers were the souls of the dead.

Yenat's mouth tightened with determination, and he spoke at last. "So you've waited until the final hour, when we are prisoners in our own city. What do you propose now, my lady?"

She smiled before replying, toying with him. "I have made my proposal, and it has been accepted. The Council and the Mage agree to a marriage of state, and to bring us the blast-powder we need." She paused, skin tingling with pleasure as a ripple of surprise ran through her listeners.

Yenat must have seen that the battle was lost, but he persisted in his opposition. "Will we not become slaves of Kir?"

"We will be no one's slaves." Without waiting for a response, Briala flung open the door to make a dramatic exit. There in the hall stood the girl Alea. Eyes wide with fright, the creature took a quick step backward. "A spy!" Briala's shout brought two Enforcers running. "Imprison her."

"But I wasn't . . . I was only waiting . . ."

Yenat hurried to the doorway. "Release her."

"And you!" Briala seized the moment to turn on him. There would never be a better time, with the remaining adepts lulled by news of the treaty with Kir. "The Fastness!"

There was a murmur of shock and some tentative objections from the other Radiants. The Fastness, unused in Briala's lifetime, was a tower room designed to hold insane or rebel adepts. Its walls were impervious to fire or sound; once locked away there, Yenat might as well be dead.

Briala waited edgily as Yenat faced his peers. "She has no right to do this!" he cried. "I have committed no wrong!"

"You have brought a spy among us," she challenged, addressing her words more to the others than to Yenat. "Can we afford trouble with the Mage coming here? If he believes there's internal dissent and that I may be overthrown, why should he marry me?"

Reluctantly the others conceded. Yenat looked for a moment as if he would fight with the deadly narrowlight at his command.

"Battle us and the girl will be tortured," Briala said. "Yield, and you may yet be restored to your position."

"And the girl?" Uncertainty. That was good.

"She may be restored also. If, indeed, there is no conspiracy."

He allowed himself to be led away. The fool actually loved his concubine. They could both rot in prison for all Briala cared.

The other adepts made way for her respectfully. Yenat had been the last to stand against her, and now he was gone.

However, the commander of the Enforcers required a meeting to discuss preparations for the Mage's arrival, and Briala was kept busy until dinnertime. That much-desired delicacy, the soul of Nle, would have to wait until tomorrow.

Following supper, she passed several hours in the school, working on the red-light. The trick of it was to channel the light through the nostrils. For a few seconds, she managed to split it, combining red-light from the nose with narrow-light from the eyes, but both were extremely weak. And so was she afterward.

No wonder the grayvers required strong young men for the tribute, Briala reflected as she made ready for bed. She stretched, yawning, trying to imagine how it would be to lie with the Mage of Kir. Was he an old man like Yenat? Had he a handsome face? If not, surely he would disguise it to please her.

That night she had the other nightmare, the new one.

Chapter Fourteen

The dream began, as always, in this same room, which was then Hakin's, on the second morning after Mera-ti had leaped into the river.

Briala entered to find her mother reading a note as a message-bird on a short tether chirped beside her. There was some conversation. Briala remembered only the gist of it, that the Council had offered a treaty against the grayvers. And Hakin meant to accept and to report the truth to them about the gift, so that they might help her destroy it.

"I want to be rid of the gift." Those words of Hakin's rang out clearly in the dream. "It writhes inside me like an alien being."

Briala saw in a flash what the future would hold for her if her mother succeeded: the real power taken by the Council, equality restored to the old race, perhaps even the bastard Mera-ti demanding to rule over the Citadel.

And more: It meant she, Briala, would grow old and decrepit, deprived of the gift that was to have been her legacy.

"How can you?" The words tore from her so vehemently that sometimes, on waking, she found herself hoarse. "You are more despicable even than father! He, at least, never took the gift for himself and then denied it to me!"

"He was right." Hakin folded the note decisively. "The tribute was wrong, a betrayal of our people. Look at Omaq, Briala! There's almost nothing left of it. Do you honestly think we hold the power?"

And turning away, Hakin began to draft her reply.

"No!" Briala snatched at the piece of paper.

"Leave the room." Hakin glared at her.

And in that instant, as their eyes met, Briala took the gift. She didn't take it, actually; it leaped to her willingly, as if it knew where it would be safe.

Without so much as blinking, Briala took something more: Her mother's soul. It pulled free of Hakin and surged into her daughter, so rich and strong that Briala could feel it transforming her, sense her body ceasing to age.

A mirror stood opposite the bed, and in it Briala saw herself transformed. She could never have said in so many words what the difference was, and yet it was unmistakable. Everything brightened, softened, grew more sensuous.

"Mother, look!" Excitedly, Briala turned and it was only then that she realized the thing on the bed was no longer her mother.

The shell stared blankly, its skin sagging. What an old woman Hakin had become, creased and sallow. Briala shuddered.

Here the dream departed from the reality. At the time, Briala had moved as if commanded from within. She knew her mother kept poison at hand, in a vial like those made for sweet fruit extract; it was that, after all, which had killed Taav. A search through the drawers turned it up, and Hakin swallowed obediently. Afterward, although some might have wondered at her sudden passing, no one seeing that wretched face doubted there had been a real illness.

But in the nightmare, someone—perhaps Yenat— came to the door while the ghoul Hakin still lived. Briala dragged the body about the room, trying to hide it under the bed or behind one of the wall coverings that had hung there at the time.

The person entered and then left. Next came the commander of the Enforcers. Somehow Hakin's body kept lurching into view, and Briala had to keep hiding it. When she thought she had gotten rid of it at last, burning it piece by piece in the fireplace, Taav's body fell out from behind the mirror.

Briala awoke covered with sweat. This was worse than the other nightmare, the old one. She had been a child then, eight, when Hakin and Taav argued after he told her of the Graylord's offer of immortality and his rejection of it.

He spoke of a responsibility to his people; Hakin accused him of cowardice. He taunted her in turn, saying he had already achieved immortality through his two daughters, and that he might bring the mutant bastard Mera-ti to live with them in the Citadel.

After he went back to his office, Briala saw her mother slip the vial of poison from a drawer and then, undecided, leave it sitting on the bureau while she stalked off her anger in the corridor.

Only Briala was present when the slave girl brought tea. Taav returned, mistook the vial for sweetener and poured a few drops in his cup. In that moment when she might have warned him, Briala, with the ferocity of a resentful eight-year-old, could think only of how her father was going to bring that other, hated daughter into his household and set her up in Briala's place.

When Hakin returned and found Taav's body, she tormented herself for days with grief. But finally she journeyed to the hills, alone, until she found the cave Taav had stumbled upon. There she sealed the bargain that ultimately led to her death.

Briala rose from bed and began to wash herself in water warmed by the hearth. Even after a night's sleep she felt tired. She needed more souls. Today one of them would be Nle's.

Once the bloodcats were fed and breakfast taken care of, Briala decided to amuse herself with Mera-ti's friend before destroying him. At her orders, he was washed, freshly garbed, and brought to her bed-chamber. He was painfully thin, and dragged one leg, Briala noted as he entered, but how those eyes burned with hatred.

He stared at her, a shade of doubt crossing his face, and Briala cursed silently. She couldn't resemble Mera-ti that closely!

"You are the Lady Briala?" he asked. "But . . . you're . . ." The words trailed away. He was fighting his attraction to her with every scant ounce of energy he possessed.

"You are not as I imagined either," she murmured. "They haven't fed you well, have they? But I expected a boy, and you're a man."

"I've grown these past few months." Bitterness resurfaced in his tone. "A lovely place to come to manhood, your prison."

Come to manhood. Yes, that he had, Briala thought, regarding the sharp planes of the face and the tense stretch of his body. With a bit more muscle, he wouldn't be ill-favored.

"I'd like to make it up to you." The words lingered between them like perfume. She traced one finger down his chest, parting the lapped robe. Nle quivered where he stood but did not answer. Briala smiled up at him and saw a muscle tighten in his jaw. Oh, what a battle he was putting up! She stood on tiptoe and her lips grazed his cheek, tracing a line toward the hard mouth.

He responded then, with a deep, almost violent kiss that stirred her. Surprisingly strong hands caught her by the waist and then, unexpectedly, pushed her away.

Caught off guard, Briala stumbled. But he wasn't finished. Nle reached over and ripped her gown halfway down the front, revealing pink-tipped breasts. "So this is what you offer," he snarled. "You're less than those poor wretches on the Street of Lost Women. Vile beneath all that glitter."

"How dare you?" Briala glared at him, at the same time aware of a liquid heat coursing through her in response to his aggression. How unfortunate that he was too dangerous. She could still induce him to couple, but he might regain his senses and injure her.

His eyes stared directly into hers. The time was ripe. Slowly, with great enjoyment, she began to suck his soul. In a flicker he recognized what was happening and fought it. But Briala's traction held, practiced and inexorable, until in a swift rush he ceased to struggle.

Oddly, she felt little sustenance. Again her gaze probed his, but met only blankness.

"What a disappointment you were, after all," she told the empty thing that stood there. "Go to the bloodcat pit and throw yourself in."

Briala turned carelessly away. The sound of a footstep was all the warning she had before cold hands grabbed her throat. She tried to scream, but the sound came out a croak. How could this have happened? He was going to kill her, clutching her from behind where she couldn't use the narrow-light on him.

Choking, seeing the world go dim, Briala arched and twisted, flinging them both to the floor. His near-starvation must have weakened him, for she managed to turn before Nle's hard, thin body covered her and he gripped her throat again. There was no reverence, no awe in the way he straddled her, like a man taking a whore.

The light wouldn't come, and the agony in her throat was all she could think about. Desperately, Briala snapped back one of his fingers, heard his gasp of pain and felt the pressure ease on her neck. She gulped in the air.

There—for a moment he had lowered his guard. She stared, caught him, and this time ignored the deceptive emptiness, plunging deeper into his being for the elusive essence.

Let him go. He's the trap we set for Mera-ti.

The voice brooked no refusal. Briala hesitated, and then she screamed.

Kah-geb rushed in, an Enforcer beside him, and together they dragged Nle off her.

"He shall be executed at once," said Kah-geb.

"No!" It hurt to talk, but she must. "Lock him in a cell apart. I have a special use for him."

Lifted to the bed and plied with finot, Briala dismissed her attendants. She wanted to be alone to commune with the voice. As soon as the door closed behind Kah-geb, she asked the emptiness, "Who are you?"

It answered with a laugh, deep and masculine.

Now she understood why Hakin had described the gift as an alien being within her. For that was exactly what it was.

The Graylord. Briala tried to recall her mother's description of him. A purple-robed mist, immensely tall, in a chamber of white fire.

A mist? Or merely a disguise?

Briala knew at once she had found the man she had unconsciously sought, the man who would be her mate. And part of him already lived within her.

Why had she ever thought the grayvers were her enemy? That was Hakin's notion, Hakin who was too weak to take this potent demon as her lord. "Are you coming here in person, coming for me?" she asked.

Oh, yes, I'm coming to Ad-Omaq.

"What about the Mage? And the blast-powder?"

You have only to open the gates for an hour, late tonight, and let us in. Then I will never leave you.

Briala lay back, remembering the coarse feel of her attacker, the rough way he'd handled her. It was the way the Graylord would make love to her.

That night she walked through the city to the gates and ordered the Enforcers away. Then she opened the portcullis to the rotting bodies that marched in silently and vanished down the shadowy streets. She felt no disgust at the sight and smell of them. Kah-geb, Yenat, Nle, all were decaying, moment by moment, everyone but her. And the Graylord.

As the days passed, she grew to feel him always with her, the resonance of his voice like a caress on her body. When she took Kah-geb to her bed, or some other Radiant or slave who caught her fancy, she imagined them to be her real lover, the Graylord.

On the seventh day, the Mage arrived in Ad-Omaq.

Chapter Fifteen

The first time Shadow saw the brown walls of Ad-Omaq and the white tower of the Citadel, a wave of fear rolled over her. After all that had happened, was she too late? If only the clarity could see into the heart of the Citadel where Nle was imprisoned, but it wasn't yet that strong. Instead, she used it to check the whereabouts of her companions, for the group was invisible.

Kirji rode in the lead on a tall harthorn, his face set in thoughtful lines. Behind him trailed Shadow, Dorf and a half-dozen Enforcers, headed by Vank. One of Kirji's counselors who had set out with them had fallen ill and gone back with three guards.

At the rear of the group trundled two dozen pack animals laden with watertight hide bags of blast-powder. Knowing what Lumle's few sticks had accomplished, Shadow suspected that this lot would shatter the caverns and a section of the mountains as well.

But what of the walking dead that had come south? Oddly, she had seen nothing of them since the Mage's small band left the forest, nor had she heard the Graylord's voice, although she still felt his chill pres-

162

ence at times. Did he know that she journeyed to Ad-Omaq? It was a great gamble, for he might seize her and use her gift to extend his power.

If only Kirji would believe her about the value of the clarity, but he continued to regard it as a clever but minor device. And the closer they drew to their destination, the more distant he became from Shadow. The feelings that had developed between them in Kir still lived in her heart and, she hoped, in his, yet circumstances had contrived to make them wary of each other.

He knows that I feel responsible for this land, that I don't want it ruled from Kir. He thinks that makes us enemies, and I can't be sure he isn't right.

Shadow shifted on her harthorn, its spine rigidly uncomfortable beneath the gaily colored quilt pad, and drew her woolen cape tighter against the sharp breeze of early winter. The air was colder on this side of the forest; Omaq lacked the warm ocean current that kept Ad-Kir springlike most of the year.

But it was her own foreboding as much as the air that chilled her. There was no telling what awaited her inside the city. Despite any assurances from Briala to the Council, Shadow's life meant nothing once the gates of Ad-Omaq closed behind her.

But if ever there was a chance to save Nle, it was now. And more than this, she sensed threads drawing together to stitch up the fate of Omaq. Lumle himself had said as much before leaving Ad-Kir, for he was not only an agent of the Council's but an adviser to them, an expert in the history of the known lands. With his heightened sense of patterns, he had agreed that the clarity, and Shadow herself, might be the key to saving her land.

Yet she felt very small, approaching the steep walls of the city, and very alone.

At least she had Dorf to aid her. And perhaps Lumle, who had hinted he might not leave the Eastern Lands immediately, but he had given no indication of what he might do after informing Briala of the Council's order, and of Kirji's acceptance.

Shadow looked up as they passed not twenty feet from a band of ghouls on the prowl. The creatures looked confused, smelling blood where they saw nothing. Breaking away, a ghoul lumbered toward them. Alarmed, Shadow's harthorn shied and stumbled, and she clutched its neck to keep from being flung off. In the struggle to regain its balance, the animal kicked a stone hard into the ghoul's face. The thing screamed and lunged blindly at them. One of the Enforcers slashed with his light-blade and brought it down.

"Are you hurt?" Momentarily lifting the illusion, Kirji reached out to steady Shadow.

His concern soothed her. "Only startled."

The group continued, speaking softly to calm the animals as, behind them, the ghoul choked out its blood and was set upon by its starving mates.

At the foot of the bridge, the Mage removed the invisibility and Vank called for entrance. The portcullis creaked upward, admitting them.

Briala had made ready, one had to grant her that. The great entrance square where Mera was executed and Shadow first met Nle sported pennants in bright reds and yellows, jutting from the windows of Highborns' stately homes. People swarmed into the square, reassured by their own numbers. And, no doubt, the Omaqi Enforcers were under orders to refrain from enslaving and murdering the citizenry in front of

Omaq's new lord, Shadow reflected with a twist of sarcasm.

She watched Kirji take in the ill-fed populace, the craven way they crept out of alleys and stood poised as if to flee. He must have seen the two children, their necks encased in metal collars, dragged on a leash by an effete Highborn male.

These people were hers. Hers as Taav's daughter, but above all because she was one of them as Briala could never be. But the power to rule was not hers; it was the Mage's. Shadow regarded him with new eyes, silently demanding that he prove himself worthy.

He took no notice of her as he stared beyond the surge of odorous humanity at the spectacle that waited across the square. A splendid throne rose above the crowd, shining like gold in the weak sunlight. Reclining upon it in a gown of ruby and a mantle of amethyst was a girl who looked much like Shadow, and nothing like her.

Briala's uptilted yellow eyes winked with youthful innocence, while the gleam of her skin and the curves visible beneath the garments radiated womanliness. Dark hair fell about her shoulders, unrestrained, as if she humbled herself before her husband-to-be. She had changed since Shadow had last seen her, as Hakin had changed years ago. This, too, was an illusion, but of a different kind from anything in Kir.

Shadow tried to trust Kirji as he rode forward to greet his bride. This was the Mage of Kir, the man who had turned a forest into a nightmare and then back into an ordinary woods again, who had bested her and most of his populace with illusion, who had cast his light into the dark corners of Shadow's heart. Surely he was not to be duped by one beautiful woman.

But she was more than that, this sister whom Shadow viewed openly for the first time. In the woman's concentrated gaze, the subtle pursing of lips and narrowing of eyes, she read a power-weaving not unlike that she herself used to draw upon the clarity.

She observed the Mage again, and saw as he rode forward that he seemed to grow taller and younger, more open and cheerful. *He's using his illusions, too.*

Perhaps, after all, it was he and not Shadow who held the key to Omaq's salvation. She must have faith in him, and hope that in the end the feelings that had grown between her and Kirji would bring them together again.

She stayed back with Dorf, although Vank and the Kirite Enforcers spurred their harthorns forward and flanked the Mage as he rode toward Briala. Kirji descended at the foot of the throne, and knelt before the seductive woman, who smiled and bade him rise. Then her gaze passed over him and across the crowd until, with a shock, Shadow realized she had been spotted.

The two sisters confronted each other across the square where so much tragedy had been played out. Shadow could feel Briala measuring her, and hating; she forced herself to display no emotion as the Mage mounted the steps to the throne.

Between her and Briala lay more than a few years of enmity, not even a lifetime of it, but rather dozens of lifetimes. It was the ancient loathing between the old race and the new, the downtrodden and the uneasily uplifted, the dark secret magic and the shallow brilliance of the light. Taav had forced them into this position, made them rivals for a father and a kingdom and a man.

Why had Briala agreed to this union? What had changed her mind since that bitter argument with Hakin?

Shadow considered using the clarity to try to read her sister's intentions but it would be too dangerous. Briala possessed light-powers of her own. Who could tell what might happen between them?

The Radiant turned her attention to welcoming Kirji, who accepted a seat beside her. Shadow couldn't hear the words of the marriage ceremony over the noise of the onlookers, but she watched the ritual unfold as the pair bowed their heads and exchanged token gifts. Afterward, the couple descended side by side into a street that led to the Citadel. Other Radiants closed around them.

"What about Nle?" Dorf asked, returning Shadow to herself.

The Kirite Enforcers were following the Mage, and she kicked her harthorn forward, not answering because she didn't yet know what the answer would be.

Kirji had declined to make any promises about seeking her friend's release until more pressing matters were resolved. She had expected this, but Shadow had no intention of waiting patiently. She would take full advantage of her opportunities as a member of the Kirite party.

Once Nle joined them, his knowledge of the city and his innate cunning would be invaluable in any plan Shadow might devise.

She had given much thought to her next steps but knew she must wait to see how the Mage proceeded. Perhaps she wouldn't need to take action. But if she did, she would have to find weapons and allies, perhaps even among the Radiants.

At the Citadel, she was helped down by slaves and escorted to a room adjoining Dorf's on the second highest level. Servants brought food and provided fresh garments and hot scented water for baths.

Cleaning herself in a large wooden tub, Shadow regarded her bedchamber. She had seen its like during her spying through the vents. Hung with tapestries, rich with brocades and furniture crafted of wizardwood, it bespoke the Radiants' wealth. The heaviness of it closed in around her like a shroud. In each stitch of brocade, she read the suffering of a peasant.

That she was here, within the Citadel, not as a prisoner but as a guest, was almost beyond belief. What were her rights, her privileges? How quickly would Briala's civility turn to savagery, and whose part would the Mage take?

Reminded of the need for haste, she finished bathing and examined the ornate dresses in the wardrobe. Probing to the back of the closet, she found a soft gray gown that suited her better than all the finery.

In the lounge-room on that level, she met Dorf and Vank. They were talking with a servant, who gaped briefly at the sight of Shadow, reminding her once again how much she resembled Briala. Recovering himself, the servant proposed to show them the sights of the Citadel, if it would please the guests of the lord and lady of Ad-Omaq. And indeed it would.

Only the highest level was barred to them, as—he explained placatingly—to all but the adepts. In unctuous tones, the fellow guided them through the artisans' workshops, pointing to colored lamps and navigational tools and other works such as Shadow had seen in Ad-Kir. She wondered that the Radiants had developed so little that was new in their years of isolation. But what need had they of invention and hard work, when their stomachs were filled by the labor of slaves?

The schoolroom held little interest for her, although Shadow knew the ground level also contained the storehouses, with their fabled wealth and, now, the blast-powder brought by the Mage. She would have liked to see those, but instead the guide led them down to the gardens.

The vastness of the enterprise was astounding. The fields must extend a considerable distance under the city. It was clear why the Radiants had run out of blast-powder, if they had used it to hollow out this space. There had been a garden here for centuries but not on such a scale. Beneath the bright artificial light sprouted field upon field of crops. This, then, explained how easily Hakin had abandoned the countryside beyond the walls of the city. She hadn't left it so much as re-created it here.

Their guide spouted volumes of information, much of it mind dulling as he enumerated the crates of vegetables produced and the bales of grain. The water, he said, came from the river and was held in a reservoir at the far side of the gardens.

Shadow scanned her surroundings with the clarity. Beyond the herds of hartbeasts and the pens and enclosures of harkbirds and nightcreepers lay the pit of the bloodcats.

As she drew back into herself, her skin prickled, and, with a shock, she felt the Graylord, felt his vast evil soul turned not toward her but toward the Mage, probing, seeking to define the newcomer's powers. But he knew Shadow was here. He had left her alone to concentrate on—Briala—*now that the bodies are in place, the growth has begun. Soon, soon . . .*

She turned to Dorf, but he was staring about, seeking his family among the stooping rows of slaves, the hundreds or perhaps thousands of peasants, many scarred and emaciated, who bent to sow the crops in one field or to harvest those in another.

She recognized one face: Argen, from the Den of Ashi, who would have helped her. He identified her in the same instant, his neck turning sharply in surprise. He looked as if he would speak, but the guide-servant was hurrying them to the dungeon.

As he unsnapped the locks on the trapdoor and pulled it open, a dark malevolence crept through the opening, unseen but felt not only by Shadow but also by her two companions. Death reigned below, not swift and merciful but slow and hideous. Death lay in wait, for her, for her. She must not enter; and yet Nle was there, if he yet lived.

Even Vank must have felt something was amiss, for he said, "You don't show these to everyone, surely?"

"We've had no visitors in the Citadel for many years." The servant called down to an Enforcer and received an echoed acknowledgment.

It seemed unlikely that Briala would be so artless as to imprison the Mage's guests. Vank's presence reassured Shadow, and she descended with the others on a ladder that, their guide explained, was pulled up during the night to make escape all but impossible.

The corridors were fiercely dark, flickering with faint light from mock torches set far apart, no doubt created in place of light globes to enhance the horror of this hole.

Vank, more stimulated than oppressed by the place,

plied their guide with questions. How many prisoners were kept here? No one knew. What crimes had they committed? From theft to murder. How long did they remain? Until they died.

"Inefficient," he observed to no one in particular.

"Does Ad-Omaq still pay tribute to the grayvers each month?" Shadow dared not inquire directly about Nle.

"No. The Lady Briala stopped that barbarism as soon as she came to power."

Vank asked, "Have you many escape attempts?"

"Only one, that I know of." The servant turned down a corridor, which snaked away beneath the low-hanging ceiling, door after identical door, tightly shut upon the wretches within. "Last month. A thin fellow with a crippled leg. The guards opened the door to admit a new prisoner and this man attacked them."

"He was killed?" Shadow's breath caught in her throat.

"No. Put in a cell by himself. There." The man pointed.

An exchange of glances told Shadow that even Dorf hadn't missed the obvious, that this tour had been arranged so Nle's cell could be pointed out to her. The story of the escape might be true or it might not, but either way it had provided an excuse to isolate Nle, for some purpose of Briala's.

Shadow concentrated. The cell was dark, but she picked out a figure limping restlessly within. Nle had grown taller in the intervening months, and he was, if possible, even thinner than before. Gently, she touched his mind, grateful for the channel that had accidentally been opened between them once long ago when she was experimenting with the clarity.

Briala—he had seen Briala—attacked—dared to attack Briala, and not been slain? Now suddenly he was aware of her probing. In a moment he would recognize that it must be Shadow, that they must not break contact yet, must make some plan—

"This way." It was the servant at Shadow's elbow, pulling her along. "Let's go up; I don't like it here."

Cursing under her breath, she climbed through the trapdoor. Only then did relief touch her: Nle was alive!

Shadow forced herself to pretend interest in the baths, which, the guide explained, were not in use since the magic heat from the earth had mysteriously vanished some weeks before. At the same time as the fire was extinguished in the Den of Ashi, no doubt, Shadow reflected wryly.

At last they were allowed to return to their rooms, and she could consider what she had learned. Nle had attacked Briala—how had that come about? Where? Above all, why did Briala want Shadow to know where he was?

Dorf came into Shadow's chamber, but they didn't dare speak freely, although the clarity showed no spies in the vents or behind the tapestries. There might be other powers of which Shadow knew nothing. She didn't believe Briala had wasted the years since the maturing of her Radiant powers.

To cover their conversation, Shadow pretended to show Dorf the new garments left for her, as if she cared for such things, and, holding a robe up to the window to show its colors, whispered, "He's there. She wanted us to know. See how the threads are of many colors, although the robe appears blue? That is the secret of its shimmering."

"How—why?" Dorf understood that a game must be played, but its complexities confounded him.

"Radiants love beautiful things; who doesn't?" Shadow set the robe aside and lifted a necklace of tiny light globes. "One could walk in the darkness with these." And added softly, "She means to trap me in an illegal act, trying to break Nle out."

"It's—lovely." Dorf still looked confused.

"Of course, I couldn't wear such things without discomfort; I bear no grudge against my sister, but the past is not so easily forgotten." Shadow handled the necklace so that the globes clinked lightly together providing a covering noise for her next words to Dorf. "I'll appeal directly to her, before Kirji. For Nle and for your family. She won't want to appear ungenerous."

"Thank you," Dorf said. "I mean—I couldn't wear such a thing, either, if—" He halted, unsure of what he meant to say.

"I want to rest now. I'll see you at supper?" Dorf nodded and went out.

Briala would, no doubt, make subtle use of the situation, of Shadow's affiliation with thieves and slaves, to weaken her in the Mage's eyes. But at least she might be caught off guard by a direct request. It was dangerous, of course, to assume anything about Briala, but two things seemed certain to Shadow.

One was that her sister didn't know the Mage's only power was illusion, and so would exert all her art to please him.

Also, the Radiant had no desire for Kirji as a man but only as a means. It was Shadow's hope, scarcely admitted even to herself, that they might observe the form of *regaja* without true intimacy.

But she must not be distracted from more important matters. The Graylord's presence had come to her strongly here in the Citadel. Had he actually traveled down from the mountains? And where were the bodies she had seen lurching through the countryside?

Again, the phrase "moving caverns" disturbed her. Was it possible the grayvers had somehow managed to transport at least some of their power base to Ad-Omaq? But how, and where was it? Surely the mountains remained their stronghold; it was there they had retreated in ages past, after the conquest of that earlier city.

She considered a dangerous tactic: to warn Briala of the Graylord's nearness and of his desire for the clarity. They might yet forge a bond between them, the two sisters. But first, she would make her request for Nle, and gauge Briala's mood by that.

Determined, Shadow commanded a servant to arrange an audience with the Mage and the Lady Briala at once.

She was told they wished to be alone together and were not to be disturbed until morning.

Chapter Sixteen

The Radiant who led Shadow to the top level the next morning was a bizarre man with breasts and an unpleasant, obsequious manner. He was, so he informed her, a cousin of Briala's on her mother's side. It was a relief to know he was no relation of Taav's.

"So, we can't wait to see the new lord and lady, can we?" said the man, Kah-geb. "Do you suppose they had a pleasant night? Must have done, I'd say."

Shadow looked around as they ascended the staircase and passed along a wood-paneled corridor much like the one on her own level. Perhaps the man was trying to bait her. She supposed her relationship with the Mage was known here, since it had been no secret in Ad-Kir.

The air of the corridor prickled at her. It was thick with past emotions. Taav had lived here, and the ancestors of Taav who were Shadow's forebears as well. Perhaps, had she leisure to use the clarity, she might learn to perceive the patterns of their days and their deaths. But such indulgence must wait.

At a double door, Kah-geb knocked briskly. Shadow smoothed out a crease in her tunic. Again, she had left the rich robes hanging in her wardrobe, this time choosing a simple garment from Kir. If nothing else, it would highlight the contrast between her and Briala.

At a muted command, she was ushered inside and the hermaphrodite was sent away.

Briala sat upon a gilded chair, her hair loose and her flowing gown in disarray. The room was not a bedchamber but an office, furnished with a desk and other finely wrought appointments. There was no sign of Kirji. For one instant, Shadow dared to use the clarity on her sister. Beneath the beauty she caught a glimpse of something white and cold, something she almost feared.

"What brings you here, Mera-ti?" Briala's voice was satiny, like the slither of an aka-serpent. She betrayed no glimmer of surprise, but then, she had been advised in advance of Shadow's request to see her.

Shadow would not kneel, but she inclined her head respectfully. "May I offer my congratulations on your marriage?"

"You may." The words carried a hint of disdain, or perhaps gloating.

Still, Shadow must attempt to gain her sister's tolerance, if not her liking. "Briala—Lady Briala—I know your mother despised me, and in a way I cannot blame her. But there is no reason for bad feeling between the two of us."

"Have I treated you ill? Have you taken offense at something?"

"No." Shadow did not like the slyness in those yellow eyes. She must conclude the interview as quickly as possible and be gone from this web. "I come to ask a favor . . ."

Kirji entered from an inner room, his silver hair rumpled and his body covered by a silken robe.

"Good morning." He studied the two of them together, and looked faintly uneasy. "Is something wrong, Shadow?"

"Shadow?" repeated Briala. "You may use the name Mera-ti without fear, if you like."

"I prefer Shadow."

"You spoke of a favor?" The Mage stopped behind and a little to one side of Briala. That he had become her lover there was no doubt, and yet he wavered, Shadow saw. How could she expect him to resist such a rare beauty who also appeared to be his ally? Yet a bond still linked him to Shadow.

"My friend Dorf," she improvised, suddenly wary, when asking for Nle, of what response her sister had prepared. "His mother and sister are slaves in the gardens. May they be freed?"

Briala's confident smile transformed into a frown. This, clearly, she had not expected. "I suppose they may."

"Why were they enslaved?" the Mage asked.

"For sleeping in the streets." Shadow hoped to remind him of the savagery of this place and of the Radiants, but her sister had a ready explanation.

"That was the law under my mother's reign. It was a means of preventing chaos, with all the peasants crowding into the city. We plan to free them, of course, but some method must be devised to insure order. But Mera-ti's friends will be released." Briala clapped her hands and, when a serving girl appeared, instructed her to see to the matter.

Instinct warned Shadow to withdraw now, without pressing the matter further. Conflicting loyalties pulled at her. Surely it was best for her people if she remained here in Ad-Omaq, free to come and go within the Citadel, maintaining at least a trace of influence on the Mage and able to gather information in bits and scratches.

By confronting Briala, she risked giving her sister some pretext to expel or imprison her. *But if I don't ask for Nle's release now, the opportunity may never come again. And Briala might just grant it, to show the Mage her generosity.*

Nle was Shadow's friend, her brother in spirit. Whatever the danger, he had first claim on her heart. Even above Kirji, although she loved him as she would never love another man.

Shadow broke the lengthening silence. "Also, my lady, I have a friend, Nle, who is held prisoner here. I ask for his release."

"And in exchange?" Briala said.

"Is he a hostage?" Shadow demanded, anger dispelling her attempt at humility.

"He has committed serious crimes, and to release him would be a large concession. When one asks such a favor, it is customary to offer a favor in return," Briala answered coolly.

"What would you ask, then?"

Briala glanced at the Mage and tapped her fingers against the arm of her chair before continuing. "You could be construed as having certain claims to the leadership of this land. Not legitimate ones, but there are troublemakers in any city, and you could provide a rallying point. I wish to prevent that."

The Mage nodded agreement. "It would be best for everyone if you were to publicly cede all claim to rule Omaq."

Anger at her own short-sightedness surged within Shadow. She had expected some devious response, and instead Briala had cut directly to the point—the one point on which the Mage obviously concurred. *I*

*shouldn't have come here today. I shouldn't have let
her bring this into the open and force my hand.*

At the same time, Shadow knew instinctively that
no declaration, however binding, would ever truly
satisfy Briala. She would find a way to have Shadow
killed.

There was no way to avoid answering, and Shadow
had no intention of renouncing the heritage that had
strengthened and challenged her since childhood, of
abandoning the people who had no one else to turn
to.

Her only chance was to speak out and hope the
Mage would be swayed.

"I would gladly give up any right to leadership if I
were confident Omaq would be ruled as it should
be." Shadow addressed herself directly to Kirji, trying
to marshal her arguments quickly. "Things are not
right within the Citadel. As I tried to tell you in Kir,
just before I fled I heard Briala and Hakin arguing,
and a few days later Hakin died suddenly. My sister
was transformed into a great beauty—you of all people should recognize illusion when you see it. She
took something from Hakin, something that Hakin
got from the grayvers. I believe they are allied."

"This is nonsense!" Briala interjected.

The Mage lifted his hand. "I wish to hear her out."

Shadow pressed on. "The Graylord is here, in
Ad-Omaq. My lord, I fear for much more than my
friends. I am afraid for this city, and for Kir and . . ."
She stopped herself, knowing he would never believe the lands beyond the ocean might also be at
risk. Instead, she finished, "and for you."

Briala's hands gripped the arms of her seat. "It's
jealousy, that's all. You see? When you told me

you'd been lovers, didn't I say she would never forgive me for marrying you?"

The tension in the room weighed heavily upon Shadow's nerves as the Mage considered. When at last he spoke, it was quietly, to her, as if they were alone.

"I think you honestly believe these suspicions are true," he said. "But I'm in a better position than you to be objective. Your perceptions are colored by resentment and, yes, jealousy. If your sister intended to side with the grayvers, why would she have made this alliance and accepted the Council's jurisdiction? No, Shadow, I must insist you renounce any claims to rule Omaq, or leave the city. I will send an escort with you to ensure your safety, of course."

Shadow stared at him helplessly. She had gambled everything and lost. "May I have a few hours to decide?"

"Very well," Kirji said. "Until this evening."

Briala's lips were pressed into a thin angry line as Shadow bowed stiffly and left. *Whatever I'm going to do, I have to do it now. And she knows it.*

"Bad news?" Kah-geb rejoined her, descending the steps with a flutter of perfume and the faint jangle of keys. "How unfortunate. But there are many pleasures to be had in the Citadel. It would, of course, be difficult to find a replacement for the Mage. But I have certain talents that could prove, shall we say, diverting?"

"I'm sure of it." Shadow was glad when he withdrew politely, as if unconcerned that his advances had been rejected.

As she strode back to her room, Shadow forced back the pain she felt over the Mage's defection. She had known even before they came here that conflict over Omaq might split them apart. And how could she expect him to believe, with only her words for evidence, that the lovely, enchanted thing called Briala was in fact guilty of hideous depravities?

Dorf had already left to seek his family by the time she regained their quarters. She understood his haste, but didn't like the separation. Now she had no way of telling him what had transpired.

Why couldn't she penetrate this mystery, even with the aid of the clarity—the reason behind her sister's offer to marry Kirji; the nearness of the Graylord; the disappearance of the walking dead? They were clues to some puzzle that ought to be plain, she felt sure, and yet she couldn't even begin to assemble it.

One thing she knew: They were in extreme danger, all of them—Shadow, Dorf, Nle, even Kirji. Especially Kirji. Well, first she must find a way to reach Nle, but how? The only way to free a prisoner here, she had determined long ago, was with a key, and . . .

Something stirred in her memory, a faint recollection of a clinking sound. The keys that jangled as Kah-geb walked. The keys to the Citadel.

Shadow sat up slowly. Kah-geb had offered his sexual attentions. She was an experienced thief, but her sister's cousin was himself an expert in intrigue. Yet, it was a chance, the only one she was likely to find in the few hours that remained to her.

If Shadow were caught, there would be no mercy. But she expected none, no matter what course she chose.

She glanced at herself in a long mirror that stood against the wall. This odd-shaped garment suited the Kirites well enough, but it looked peculiar by Omaqi standards. She searched through the gowns in the wardrobe. A dark blue velvet robe enhanced her vivid coloring, although it was cut lower than Shadow liked. It came with a small round cap that fastened in the hair with glittering clips, perhaps a tactful way of encouraging her to keep the horns out of sight.

The only suitable sandals were thin and silvery. They would get in her way if she had to make a dash for it, she noted irritably, but she could hardly wear her walking-boots.

A servant carried her message to Kah-geb and, returning, ushered her up to his suite. His chamber was sumptuous to the point of clutter, swaddled in silk hangings and crowded with heavy furniture. Colored-glass lamps bulged on the tabletops, two bronze statues of harthorns bordered the bed and a swathe of golden material rippled across the ceiling.

"I'm glad you reconsidered." The hermaphrodite greeted her from beside a small table, where he poured out two glasses of finot. Shadow took hers with thanks but drank nothing until she saw him sip from his own goblet.

"Forgive my ill temper this morning." She chose a seat on a curving couch. "My experiences with men are somewhat limited."

"All the better." Kah-geb wiped a drop of liquid from his lips. He wore a heavily embroidered jacket and trousers that would have brought a fistful of silver coins from a thief-trader. "The dress becomes you." He reached over to finger the material. "Would you be offended if I observed that there's a striking resemblance between you and your sister?"

"I wouldn't, but she might."

"She might indeed." He laughed dryly. "Briala doesn't like being compared to anyone. She considers herself unique in the universe. And perhaps she is."

Shadow guided the discussion away from such dangerous grounds, questioning the hermaphrodite about amusements in the Citadel and only half-listening to the answers as he sat beside her. The keys were no longer on him; he had placed them on the table before making himself comfortable. He was chattering of Briala again, of how they had been such close friends in the past but were so no longer, now that she had a husband. How could she take the keys without his noticing? Finot did not dull the mind—

"Have you some stronger drink?" Shadow asked. "Or perhaps you don't like it."

"I? Indeed, I chose finot because I thought it would be to your taste. It's Briala's favorite; but, of course, you are not alike." He provided them each with a goblet of something fierce and bitter, and Shadow had to strain against a fit of coughing when she tasted it. She dared drink only a little. They sipped and talked; his hand traced her body, and she disguised her revulsion, smiling at him and mimicking as best she could her sister's way of moving.

In close proximity, his grotesque body seemed almost clownish, but it would be most unwise to underestimate one who had survived so well in this serpent's pit of a Citadel. Shadow began to question the wisdom of her plan. Determined though she might be, she doubted she could mislead the creature as to her physical responses. She had already acted without thinking carefully once today, and had thus played into Briala's hands. Was this, too, a miscalculation?

Someone rapped on the door. With a muttered oath and an apology to Shadow, the hermaphrodite answered it. A Highborn woman waited just outside in the corridor, and they spoke in low tones.

Her breath catching in her throat, Shadow walked to the table as if to pour herself another drink. With the silence of a city-sneak, she swept the keys into her billowing sleeve.

At the door, the woman's voice rose in anger. She had been denied some privilege she considered her due; as Briala's secretary and, apparently, as the woman's occasional lover, Kah-geb must assist her. His annoyance was plain, but at last he turned to Shadow. "My most sincere regrets, Mera-ti, but duty calls me away. Would you return this evening, when we can resume our—friendship—without interruption?"

"Of course." How soon would he notice that the keys were missing? She murmured a farewell and walked away steadily, not letting the keys scrape.

There was no time to stop by her room to change clothing; the theft might be discovered at any moment. Shadow moved down the steps slowly, trying not to attract attention. She passed her own level, and the artisans' floor. Several Radiants acknowledged her with a nod or a word of greeting. One called her "My Lady," and she realized they had mistaken her for Briala.

For once the resemblance between them might serve a useful purpose, Shadow reflected as she passed through the schoolrooms and down to the next level.

The response from the slaves as she crossed the gardens was quickly hidden, but she felt their hatred. Then she recognized a face: Argen. Did he notice the masquerade? Shadow searched the fields urgently for Dorf. But she saw no sign of the large man, and it was too late to delay any longer.

An Enforcer admitted her to the dungeon without question. Was Briala in the habit of coming here alone? Her throat constricting, Shadow retraced her steps of the previous day to Nle's cell. She made certain of her way with the clarity, adding a quick examination of her surroundings to ensure that no one else was approaching.

Shadow fumbled with the keys. There were nearly a dozen, and she had to force steadiness into her hand as she tried them. Then one caught and turned, and she strained to pull the door outward. Wrenching it open a crack, Shadow slipped inside. "Nle?"

A thin figure darted to his feet. "More of your tricks, Briala?"

"It's me. Shadow!"

He peered closely in the dim light and then two wiry, strong arms swept her against him. "Shadow. My friend. What are you doing here?"

"We have to go."

"Dorf?"

"In the gardens. I couldn't wait."

"It's all right." Nle held her close a moment longer, like a man drinking from a well after a long dry journey. "Well?"

"The Enforcers mistook me for Briala."

Nle shook his head. "It might get us out of prison, but not through the Citadel, not with me along. We'll have to swim through the reservoir. It's connected to the river—"

Footsteps clicked in the corridor. Two men, perhaps, and one woman.

Nle tightened his grip on Shadow's arm as the door swung open. Briala stood there, flanked by Kah-geb and an Enforcer. "How neatly you followed where you were led." She turned to the guard. "Take the prisoner Nle and kill him. He is of no further use to us."

"The Mage . . ."

"He'll believe what I tell him." Briala paused until the Enforcer had dragged Nle from the cell. "It will be very convincing, how you attacked me, and I struck in self-defense. A blow to the head—how unfortunate. Kah-geb, leave us alone together."

"But, cousin, she could be dangerous . . ."

"Alone!"

Shadow watched coldly as he stepped out of the cell. She had known her risks. Twice in one day, she had lost. But perhaps there was some yet-unsuspected use for the clarity, some defense. . . .

"I'll do you one last favor, sister." Briala spat the word as if it were an insult. "I'll tell you why you're dying, what I will take. Your gift, with all its uses; and your soul, to be made and unmade again, a living death. Don't try to clear your mind. We know that trick."

Her eyes fastened upon Shadow's, but it was not Briala who looked through them. It was a vast white world of frozen waste, a deathlord whose power wrenched Shadow's soul from her body, reverberating through the dungeon with dark, triumphant laughter.

Chapter Seventeen

Mist rolled through Shadow, blanking out her awareness of anything but a white world pulsing through a red haze. She could smell the blood flowing through her sister's veins. Blood like finot. How it would warm, satisfy, exhilarate.

Then Shadow's ghoul-hunger snapped, and she was returned to herself. Someone had grabbed Briala from behind, a thick arm choking the delicate neck. Dorf! No, not Dorf, but a woman his size, a look of concentration puckering her round face. At last, in her fierce grip, Briala ceased struggling and hung limply.

"Shadow?" The Dorf-shaped woman let Briala sag to the floor. "I'm Enra, Dorf's sister."

"Is Nle?"

"Here." To her relief, her friend appeared behind Enra. "Argen keeps his eyes open. Kah-geb and the Enforcer are dead. And her?"

Shadow felt Briala's pulse, faint but steady. "Alive, but barely."

"I'll see to that."

But as he knelt, Argen's voice called a warning. Enforcers! They're coming through the fields!"

Nle hesitated beside Briala's body, hands flexing, but Enra pulled him away. "She won't die quickly, that one."

Shadow checked frantically with the clarity. There was only one exit from the dungeon, dangerous as it might be. She ran after the others, Dorf and Argen, Enra and Nle, down the corridor and up the ladder.

The Enforcers stumbled back in confusion as five people, two of them giants, burst into their midst. In a flurry of blows and thrusts of Argen's knife, the outcasts battled their way free before the Enforcers' weapons could be drawn.

The first ray shot wild, searing the ground near Shadow's foot as she ran. But it would only be seconds before the fiery light cut her.

Shouting erupted behind them, interspersed with the whirr of weapons, but nothing flared toward the fleeing band. Shadow risked a glance back. A throng of field-slaves mobbed the Enforcers with screams of pent-up rage, as if some long-muttered, formless wish to rebel had ignited spontaneously.

As Shadow watched, a beam caught one of the peasants in the chest, enveloping his body in a shock of light before he blackened and collapsed.

"Come on!" Argen reached for her.

Shadow shook her arm free. "I can't leave them to die."

Dorf blocked her. "All you'll do is die with them, or hand yourself over to the Graylord."

The Graylord. He had looked at her through Briala's eyes. He was close, a cold breath upon her neck. With a shudder, Shadow turned and joined the others as Argen led them on a dodging trail through the pens and barns toward the reservoir, a path he must have marked out in his mind over the past weeks.

Shadow scanned the expanse and her last faint hope withered. "The pipe to the river—it's too narrow. Dorf and Enra could never get through."

"Leave us," Dorf said.

"No. We'll take the main staircase and pretend I'm Briala." Lifting her chin in an approximation of her sister's bearing, Shadow strode ahead without giving them time for a response. The barns shielded them from the Enforcers' view until they reached the stairs, where more Enforcers and some Radiants rushed by, heading down to the battle.

"My Lady! You are retreating?" demanded a wrinkled woman, her yellow eyes dull with age.

"Kah-geb is in command below. I must fetch the Mage." Shadow pushed by her, hearing a subdued "Oh, yes, of course," as the woman drew back. The upward flight continued in all its feigned arrogance, step by measured step. From below came screams, and the smell of flesh charring beneath light-weapons, and Shadow wept in her heart.

They reached the ground level, moved into the schoolrooms and toward the entrance hall. From nowhere a hand gripped Shadow's shoulder. The Mage materialized, his turquoise eyes dark with fury. "What have you done to Briala? Answer me!"

"She's alive." Shadow answered as calmly as she could, still hoping that somehow she could make him see reason. "Kirji, Briala tried to take my soul for the Graylord. You've been tricked."

"By her or by you?" Doubt warred with suspicion in his eyes. "How do I know it isn't you who serves the Graylord?"

At that moment Enforcers surged up the stairs, and there was no time to answer him.

Shadow lunged away with her friends as streams of

light flamed after them. In the vast entrance hallway, luck was with them. The great doors had been opened to admit three Highborn women and their servants. The outcasts dove through, scattering the startled women.

Nle limped badly, and Dorf and Enra caught him up between them as they jagged through the streets. The Enforcers dared not shoot without a clear aim, for these houses belonged to Highborns. But the pursuit was quick, and the city itself a fortress. They had to get out of sight, and there was only one way to do that, in the sneakways of Ad-Omaq.

The clarity showed an alley where the ground gaped open. Ashi would have repaired it at once, but he was no longer there to protect his Den. They dropped through and plunged into the muck, skidding along the sewer labyrinth. Shadow's velvet gown caked around the hem, hampering her. She had lost her flimsy sandals in the flight, and now mucked barefoot through the ooze.

Their pace slowed as they heard no one following and the clarity revealed no stalkers. Possibly the Enforcers were needed in the Citadel, and Kirji would have gone after Briala. But this respite would surely be brief.

With Argen's knife, Shadow hacked off her skirt at the knee and tied the extra fabric around her feet. Then, at a steadier pace, they went on.

How long ago it seemed since she had fled through here with the bloodcat in pursuit. Once she entered the safe harbor of Kir and surrendered to the Mage's charms, Shadow had never expected to find herself in these slimepits again. But at least she was among friends, whatever might come to them in the end.

Nle broke the silence as they trudged downward, taking branch courses to confuse those who would follow. "Dorf, where's your mother?"

"She was too weak. No use to them." The giant spoke with unaccustomed bitterness.

"The worn-out slaves are fed to the bloodcats," Argen said.

Shadow recalled the confrontation in the cell. "Briala must take their souls first, like a ghoul."

They followed Argen's lead to a side cavern where, months before, he had hidden a cache of food in a crevice. Well-wrapped against moisture, the dried meat and crackers were still edible, although meager when divided by five.

Argen kept to himself, chewing his small rations without complaint. He still wanted Shadow; she felt it whenever he looked at her. But there could never be another man after Kirji.

As she finished her portion, it came to Shadow that no one wanted to speak the truth. Which was that, between the grayvers and the Radiants, there could be no escape, not for them nor for anyone else in Ad-Omaq. The Mage and his Enforcers had marched into a death-trap, on orders of the Council.

Yet that she should be captured, that the clarity should be taken by the Graylord was unthinkable. It would give him the power to renew himself endlessly, to spread his dominion beyond the sea. If she were to die here, by her own hand, among friends, such conquest would be impossible.

But if Lumle had been correct, if the clarity born of the old race and the Radiant-power held the solution to defeating the grayvers, then Shadow's death would doom Omaq and Kir to desolation.

Her thoughts turned to Lumle. He had said, upon leaving Ad-Kir for the Citadel, that he might not go directly home after delivering the message to Briala. Where could he have gone, and to what end?

She had to keep fighting, however hopeless it might seem. But first she had to stay alive.

Her companions stirred restlessly, the meal finished. Shadow told them how she had descended past the Den of Ashi and leaped into the river; they concurred that there seemed no other course. At least in open countryside they might have a slim chance of survival.

They kept watch as they slogged downhill, but there was no indication of pursuit, not even the murmur of the Graylord in Shadow's mind. And, of course, the Radiants would need light to follow the trail left by the fugitives, enough illumination to reveal their approach from some distance away.

But the quiet left Shadow uneasy. Since her escape, had the Radiants made changes in the sewers, ones that even the clarity could not detect? Briala wouldn't have let her Radiant powers lie fallow. She might have found some new use for them, some new weapon, honed and ready for such a challenge as this.

Concentrating as she was on the danger from the Radiants, Shadow spared no thought for the larger puzzle nor for the mysterious disappearance of the walking dead, not until she came around a curve in the sewers and halted in the sludge.

Bodies sprawled across the sewer ahead, knees and shoulders jutting from the muck. There were men, women, children, some with slashed throats, others with crushed skulls or gashes on their bodies.

The smell of putrefaction rushed in upon her, violent and stomach-wrenching, and yet the lyworms had barely begun to penetrate. These wretches had been long dead but they had not lain here in the sewers for more than a few days.

One body had been torn completely open, and from it something had splattered against the wall. Something that glowed faintly. White radiance, without warmth; mold from the mountains, mold from the Graylord's cavern, mold that grew back when dislodged. Mold that consumed, that twisted itself, that had become a parasite on more than cave walls: a parasite on the earth, on man—

Shadow felt its pulsing life, its centuries of devising, its inhuman knowing. She felt the shapes within it, the shapes projected into the world. This, then, was what the grayvers were, not beings at all, but creatures of the mold, reflections of its evil essence. Until now, it had grown only within the caves and been limited by them, but now it had been carried to the sewers of Ad-Omaq, to make itself a second home, to multiply and feed upon the city.

She explained her discovery as best she could to her companions. Asked where the grayvers were, she could only say, "Wherever they want to be. Someone has let these bodies into the city; it had to be Briala. She's the only one with enough authority to do whatever she wants."

Argen absorbed it first. "With a base in Ad-Omaq, the grayvers could reach ships in the sea, perhaps Ad-Kir as well."

Even without the clarity, the Graylord has set his conquest well in motion. A tale Lumle had told came back to Shadow. "The grayvers conquered Omaq before, in legendary times. They destroyed an ancient city, down to the last stone, and all the people."

"But the old race survived," said Enra.

Like her brother, Enra had the gift of simplicity. That the old race had endured meant that the grayvers' conquest hadn't been complete, and that fact could be highly significant. If Shadow had more time to ponder—but first she must check the caverns for pursuers.

The clarity came into focus with no effort on her part. The Radiants were indeed tracking them now, guided through the sewers by a faint red luminescence barely perceptible to normal eyes. This must be Briala's device for finding her prey in darkness.

Shadow's mind flicked along the maze of passageways. Other Radiants approached, again using the red-light. With it, they could have crept up unnoticed upon almost anyone; anyone but Shadow, and even upon her, if she were any less watchful.

She pressed the clarity to find some unblocked route, and it responded sharply, showing her the Den of Ashi. It lay between them and their hunters, and there was a way out. Of course! Ashi had to have some means of fetching the finot and the food he served. Quickly, Shadow led her group along one twisting passage after another, ignoring the mire that pulled at her legs.

The Den had been smashed to piles of splintered wood and clean-picked bones. Shadow raced into a side corridor and struck the panel hidden beneath tendrils of moss. A thick chunk of wall dislodged itself, half-opening until there was room for one person to pass. They squeezed through, Dorf last of all, opening a gash in his shoulder as he forced his way in and then swung the secret door back into place.

It had long been rumored in the underworld that there existed a twin to the sewers, a network of narrow passageways build for workmen in the early days of the city, to service the sewers. During the long neglect, these had fallen into disuse and the entranceways had been forgotten or, more likely, sealed off by Ashi and his forebears.

Slowed by the blackness, Shadow found the way up a cramped staircase carved in the rock. Behind them, the clarity showed Radiants gathered in the Den, searching its tuberous offshoots in vain. Bloodcats might have sniffed out the secret, but they hadn't been brought, perhaps because their noise might dispel any advantage from the red-light.

Shadow continued upward past level after level, until the staircase ended at a hinged door in the roof, around which teased hints of light. With the clarity, she saw that they stood beneath the Radiants' storehouse, which sprawled on the ground level of the Citadel, in a section far from the comings and goings of the entrance. Its legendary wealth had spawned many fruitless plots in the filthholes of Ad-Omaq. And all along, this all-but-forgotten access must have permitted Ashi to raid the place at will.

With the combined strength of Dorf, Argen and Enra, they managed to lift the panel and, making sure there were no Enforcers about, crawled through.

Before them stretched room after room of such riches as Shadow had never seen gathered together: light-globes, glow-gems, vast stores of food and finot, silks and lace and harthorn leather; medication for Dorf's wound; anything she had ever dreamed of in her days as a thief.

They feasted, kicking aside the munts that squeaked underfoot, for in their wealth the Radiants had grown careless. When it came time to rest, the fugitives sought a room without food so as to be free of vermin, and were pleased to find a chamber piled with soft bags made of harthorn-hide. Mounding up bags to hide behind, the band made themselves a nest and posted a guard.

As Shadow sank into sleep, vague images spun through her head. The Mage's caravan, wending its way to Ad-Omaq with its load of blast-powder. The ghastly bodies in the sewers, spilling mold onto the walls. Enra pointing out that the old race had survived the destruction of their city, although not a stone was left. . . .

Shadow sat up abruptly, sleep retreating to the edges of her consciousness and taking with it the thought she had nearly grasped. She *must* remember. Blast-powder. The grayvers. The old race . . . "The ancient city!" The sound of her own voice startled her. She hadn't known she was speaking aloud. "The grayvers didn't destroy it; the people did!"

Around her, the others mumbled into wakefulness, rolling over to listen. Nle slid down from his guardpost atop the bags as Shadow spilled out her realization.

Once before, the grayvers must have transported their mother mold and infested the old city with it. But they had not, as Lumle believed, killed all the people, for the old race had lived on. Neither would the grayvers have tumbled the city into ruins, for it was in the protected darkness of its byways that the mold flourished. It must have been the people who tore the city down, smashed it themselves with whatever tools they had in those times, and by doing so they'd forced the grayvers back to the mountains.

And now, in the storehouse of the Radiants, Shadow and her friends lay amidst bags and bags of the thing the ancients had not possessed, the thing Briala had no intention of using against the grayvers and so had carelessly stored here. With the blast-powder the Mage had brought, Shadow and her friends had stumbled upon one last chance to stop the grayvers.

Chapter Eighteen

The laying of blast-powder was not to be a simple matter, Shadow quickly discovered. Without knowing all the properties of the stuff, her friends must find a way to undermine the city with it, and set it off without injury to themselves or to any more of the people of Ad-Omaq than necessary.

They discovered on opening the sacks that the powder was compressed into sticks roped together to permit firing from a wick. Methodically, the band began to organize, securing sparkers from elsewhere in the storehouse, laying out as best they could a map of the city, attempting to calculate how much powder would be needed at each juncture of the sewers. Double strands must be laid, in case some failed to fire; the excess would be left in the Citadel for a final, crowning blast.

It became clear that the fuses could not all be fired from one central point. Each member of the band would have to be responsible for a sector, both for laying the blast-powder and setting it off. A sequence was established to permit them to escape toward the main gate, which would be demolished last.

Only Shadow dared enter the vents and, keeping

watch with the clarity, lay powder in the walls of the Citadel. Nle chose the next most dangerous sector, nearby; since it would be too perilous for Shadow to remain inside the Citadel, he could fire her fuses along with his own. Argen and Enra would take larger areas of the sewers farther away, and Dorf was given the region closest to the main gate.

A sticking point proved to be how to warn the people of Omaq so that they wouldn't panic and run blindly to their own destruction. The danger in any warning was that it might reach the Radiants and betray the plan. At last it was decided to tell whatever people they encountered to head for the forest "when the time comes."

"Let's hope the tongues of Ad-Omaq wag fast enough," Argen said grimly as they set the time of detonation for dawn of the following day.

There was one to whom no word could be sent: the Mage of Kir. But Shadow vowed silently to make one final effort to get him out of the city.

They didn't dare begin their work until nightfall and so, keyed up by what awaited them, the conspirators rested uneasily throughout the day.

Argen was standing guard when Shadow awoke. After a hurried meal, supplies and knapsacks were distributed and her four friends descended into the tunnels again. They were hoping that the Radiants would expect the fugitives to put as much distance as possible between themselves and the Citadel; in some ways, it might be those who ranged farthest beneath the city who would encounter the greatest danger.

One matter especially troubled Shadow. The grayvers must have reached Ad-Omaq along with the mold, yet so far there had been no sign of ghoul-making in the streets. The Gray Ones were being held back. She could only guess at the reason: that the Graylord and Briala still were unsure of the Mage's true powers and didn't want to alarm him until they were certain they would prevail.

The clarity showed that Shadow's long-ago foray through the vents had caused the Radiants to screen off the system where it opened onto a side street. But apparently neither Hakin nor Briala had considered that the vents might be penetrated from within the Citadel.

Shadow entered without difficulty from the storehouse, and decided to start at the lowest level, the prison, where any noise she made would go unheeded except by prisoners. For several hours she placed powder-sticks, carrying them with her in a rough bag and whispering the warning into each cell. Sometimes she was answered with a puzzled thanks but more often with a curse, or silence.

Unable to bear as heavy a burden as Dorf and Enra and Argen—and further hampered by the need to squeeze through the narrow pipes—Shadow was forced to return several times to the storehouse for more supplies. Once she encountered Nle, whose lameness also hampered him. He reported having barely escaped an Enforcer, but he didn't think the man had recognized him or spotted the powder-sticks.

Shadow's next challenge was to warn the slaves, many of whom slept in the fields under guard and would no doubt be more closely watched than ever after the morning's rebellion. Moreover, the bloodcats napped restlessly in their pit, alert even in sleep to unaccustomed scents and sounds.

Gazing from the vents, she spotted signs of damage in the gardens, although the revolt had obviously been quelled. One of the barns lay burned and empty, and the ground near the trapdoor was dark with blood. Shadow saw no one she could address without having to shout, except a small boy climbing from a pile of broken tools in which he must have hidden hours before, during the fighting. No older than six or seven, he might misunderstand and give the alarm, but the chance must be taken.

She called to him softly. Beyond the livestock pens, a bloodcat grunted. The tousled head turned, eyes wide. She gestured the boy over and, too frightened to refuse, he edged closer. "Listen to me: you must say nothing to the Enforcers." Shadow hoped the child heard her words and not just an eerie voice from the wall. "Tell the others: when the time comes, go to the forest. Can you remember that?"

"When the time comes, go to the forest," he repeated.

"Good. Now go tell them." The child took off at a run. An Enforcer glanced at him for one heart-stopping instant, then went back to playing at tiles with a companion.

Shadow had failed to save the boy in Migal's troupe. Perhaps this time there'd be better luck.

She continued laying powder up pipes adjacent to the entrance level, cursing the now-ragged dress which tangled about her legs and left her shoulders bare to the cold. At times she felt something stir in the gray space in her mind, and waited, hoping to feel something of the Graylord, perhaps to hear words that might tip his plans to her. The channel that had opened during their contact in the caves was proving, Shadow reflected, to be more to her benefit than his. But nothing came.

She worked her way up through the levels of the Citadel. Although it must be very late by now, she heard movement and low voices as she moved from place to place. Some were lovers' trysts, while others signaled plots within plots to gain power in the Citadel, spurred by Kah-geb's death, for someone must take his place as the Lady Briala's secretary. And there was widespread speculation about the Mage and the fugitives, or so it seemed from the fragments of conversation she overheard.

Finally Shadow reached the tower, where she looked in at an odd room, windowless and lined with metal. A prison, but why here in such isolation, and who was the man pacing restlessly within? He wore Radiant's robes, and as she watched an arc of light sizzled from his eyes to jolt uselessly against the door. An enemy of Briala's? Even so, that might not make him a friend of the rebels. She gave him no warning; not only out of mistrust, but because locked away in this high place, he could make no use of it.

The powder-laying completed, Shadow moved down through the pipes to peer into Briala's chamber. Dawn was still some time away. If ever the Mage were to be saved, it must be now.

At first she thought the room was empty. Then something stirred in the vastness of the bed, and a silvery head appeared. Beside the Mage, Briala emerged, stretching sinuously. Her husband watched as she arched her back, accentuating the lushness of her body.

"You know," the artful woman murmured, "I understand why you hesitate to turn against Mera-ti. But she must be captured, you do see that, don't you?"

Kirji's eyes seemed to focus on some distant image. "Let her go, Briala. She can do you no harm now."

"No harm?" Briala's voice started to rise, and it was with a visible effort that she recaptured her languorous tone. "But think what mischief she might make if she reaches the Council!"

"How can she reach them, across the ocean?" His hand ruffled lightly through his wife's gleaming dark hair. "Briala, give up this hatred of Mera-ti. It's poisoning you, and we have more urgent business. I must leave for the mountains at once, tomorrow if your guard can spare enough Enforcers."

"You take her side, then?" Briala pouted with feigned childishness. "Haven't I given you the best nights of your life? Don't you know that I love you endlessly?"

"You're the most beautiful creature I've ever seen." There was a tautness in Kirji's voice, as if he struggled against himself. "When I'm with you, Briala, it's hard for me to think of anything else. But we must be reasonable. Your sister—"

"I'll tell you what!" Briala gave a little bounce on the bed as she turned toward him. "Catch her for me and I promise not to hurt her. I'll just keep her here until everything's taken care of, and then you can send her back to Kir, or anywhere you want."

The Mage's expression softened into a smile. "What makes you so sure I can catch her?"

"With all those powers of yours?" Briala fluttered at him. "Don't think I haven't heard the old stories! Of course, you've shown me powers I *hadn't* heard about"—she giggled suggestively, an irritating noise that made Shadow want to slap her—"but surely you could capture her with one wave of your hand, if you wanted to."

It seemed to Shadow that lights must flash across the room to warn of danger, or some voice cry out.

Surely the peril was evident, even to Kirji. But the power that infested Briala had beguiled him past caution.

"I only wish it were that easy." He shrugged regretfully. "The invisibility has many uses, of course, and illusions have kept the forest closed all these years. But not to Shadow. With her gift, Briala, she can see through them."

"I don't understand." The ruler of Omaq sat straight up among the bedcovers, staring at him. "Are you saying all you have are illusions?"

"All?" Kirji repeated. "I've never thought of them as something minor. Briala, the Kirites have grown powerful on the strength of illusions."

The woman was no longer listening as she arose and dressed hurriedly. "There's someone I must speak with." She paused before the mirror to straighten her dress, which glittered with the gold threads wove through it. "No, don't come with me. I'll only be a moment."

"The Citadel may not be safe at this hour, even for you." The Mage rose from the bed, pulling on a silver robe. "I'll come."

"No!" There was no mistaking the disdain in her tone. "I can manage my own affairs."

"Briala, have I offended you?"

"No—yes!" She stood in the doorway and confronted the Mage. "Always when I speak of Mera-ti, you take her part. You refuse to see that she hopes to destroy me, and you as well. I might almost think you were in love with her, you're so blind to the truth."

"I don't mean to take her part, but I have to be fair." Clearly disturbed by her accusation, the Mage reached for Briala, but she pulled away.

"Forget she was your lover! You're my husband now," Briala snapped. "If your illusions have any power to find and capture her, then do it." Before he could respond, she stepped through the door and closed it firmly behind her.

The Mage hesitated, then sank into a chair. Now. Now was the time to reach him, before Briala returned; before she could communicate with the Graylord, and seal Kirji's fate.

There was no way out through the narrow vents in this room. Hurriedly, Shadow crept along the pipes, using the clarity to find a larger opening farther down the hall, inside a closet. Briala's suite would be to her right, Kah-geb's to her left. The one that used to be Kah-geb's.

The hall was empty. Still, Shadow's senses stirred as she prowled along the corridor. Was it the contact with the mold that had sensitized the clarity to the point of confusion? Others had walked this path and she saw them faintly, moving with her, against her, across her. Taav and Hakin, other Radiants, and some servants as well. People of her parents' generation, and from earlier times. They whispered to each other of emotions buried and forgotten as they hurried toward destinations long vanished. Shadow could only hope her fragmenting concentration wouldn't overlook some real presence.

The ghosts in the hallway were forgotten the instant she pushed open the door to Briala's room. Across from her, the Mage froze. In his momentary confusion, she saw that he had thought her to be Briala and wondered at her unkempt state.

Before he could recover, she said, "I had to warn you. Now that Briala knows illusions are your only gift, you're at the mercy of the Graylord." When there was no response, Shadow pressed on despite her growing uneasiness. "They'll take your soul, Kirji, Please, you mustn't still be here when she comes back."

He shut his eyes for one tortured moment and then, looking past her to the open door, called, "Guards!"

Even as Shadow turned to run, Vank and three Enforcers dashed forward to block her escape.

"Hold her until the Lady Briala returns," said the Mage.

Chapter Nineteen

Stunned, Shadow made no protest as the Enforcers pulled her down the corridor and through a door. As it closed behind them, she realized they were in the chambers that had been Kah-geb's. The Enforcers in their plain green uniforms looked odd against the effete sumptuousness of the apartment.

Vank's voice was low and relentless. "Is the Mage in danger?" He watched her sharply, as if through sheer will he could detect any dishonesty.

"Briala belongs to the Graylord. Now that they know the Mage has no power but illusion, they'll toss him aside like rubbish."

Vank signaled and one of the other men flipped open her knapsack, knocking out a string of powder-sticks. "What's this for?"

It wouldn't take him long to figure it out if he put his mind to it so she spared him the effort. "For blowing up the Citadel."

"You mean to kill the Mage yourself?"

"I was trying to warn him." Quickly, she described the danger, saying as little as possible of the plan so that her friends might still have some chance of escape if Vank informed the Radiants.

Listening, he shook his head uncertainly, his young face heavy with the need for decisions beyond his experience. One of the other Enforcers spoke in her behalf, an older man, reminding Vank that only that morning the Lady Briala had suggested the Mage send his Enforcers home and rely on hers. "He hasn't been himself since we came here. If you ask me, he's bewitched."

"We'd better alert him at once. If he knew of these spore-filled bodies, he might change his mind." Vank took one guard with him, leaving two to watch Shadow. She hoped the Mage would at least listen to his own men.

The remaining guards politely turned aside as Shadow shed her disheveled gown for a short robe of Kah-geb's and a thick cloak, and tied back her tangle of hair. She washed her feet in a bowl of scented water and selected the smallest, sturdiest pair of shoes from the wardrobe, stuffing them with silken handkerchiefs until they fit.

As she was finishing, Vank and his accomplice slipped in. They had arrived too late: Briala had returned, and the door was barred. Vank's instinct to smash it had been tempered by common sense, since the Radiant could flame them in an instant with her light-skills.

"You must use this gift of yours," Vank said. "Tell me what's going on in there. If the danger is immediate, we'll break in, whatever the cost."

Shadow focused and found Briala gloating as the Mage told her of Shadow's capture. Then other figures superimposed themselves in the chamber. She saw the child-Briala watch as Taav drank something and collapsed. Taav; had he truly been murdered, or was this some trick of the Graylord's? She must not be distracted. The Mage. Where—she couldn't find him—there, sprawled across the bed, unmoving—Briala laughing, a cold cruel mirth, spinning an illusion, a dim semblance of Hakin, and then abandoning the room without another glance.

Frightened, Shadow told what she had seen. The Enforcers raced along the corridor and into the chamber. Kirji lifted his head bleakly as they dashed in and stared at them with white eyes.

Vank shook his lord violently, but the eyes remained vacant. "We should have fought. We should have killed the filthy bitch."

Before, there had at least been the possibility that Kirji might be won back. Now he was gone. But so had Ashi been. . . .

Past him, out the window, the three moons sank toward the horizon. The other conspirators would be moving stealthily to their firing-points. The fuses must be lit at sunrise, no matter who was missing.

"In less than an hour, this city will be blasted to rubble." Shadow's voice seemed to come from some stranger's throat.

Vank roused from his grief. "Then we must get out, and quickly."

The ghoul Kirji began to rouse. Swiftly, the Enforcers bound the body of their Mage and concealed him in a blanket. Outside the room, by the staircase, Shadow remembered the man imprisoned in the tower. As a rebel Radiant, he might yet prove of value. With one of the guards, she raced up, but as they pried off the bolt, a tongue of fire lashed out through a crack in the door and they left the man to work off what remained of the fastening under his own power.

At this early hour, the empty staircase echoed with their footsteps and occasionally a snarl from the ghoul beneath its blanket. Omaqi Enforcers were stationed at each level, but they accepted Vank's curt report that Shadow was being taken to prison.

On the ground level, they found the portals to the Citadel sealed for the night. These were controlled from a booth high overhead, manned by an Enforcer captain who had pulled his rope ladder up with him. From where they stood in the darkness of the hall, he was plainly visible, resting on his platform, unsuspecting of any peril. Shadow flattened herself to one side as the rest of the group proceeded forward.

"Halt!" Roused at last, the captain leaned over to inspect them.

Vank saluted. "We are under orders from the Mage. Let us pass."

"What are you carrying there?"

Vank reached under the blanket, and drew out his weapon. Before the Omaqi could respond, a beam of fire hurtled his body to the floor.

Shadow began to climb. The stone surface was rough and creviced, full of footholds for a trained sneak-thief. Vank and his men dwindled below her. How soon would Briala find her prey missing and raise the alarm? If she had mastered the illusion-power. . . . Shadow tried to use the clarity to check the hall for invisible attackers, and nearly slipped and fell. But at least she saw no hidden figures below.

Finally, drenched in sweat, she crawled out onto the ledge. The door mechanism proved to be a hefty metal wheel, and Shadow struggled to turn it. The doors groaned but held. She threw her entire body

into the effort, wrenching until her arms strained at
their sockets. The wheel shifted. With a loud scrape,
the great doors slid apart, leaving a crack barely wide
enough for a man to pass through.

Shadow scurried down, trying not to think about
the drop that faced her at any misstep. Outside the
door, Vank and his men waited for her to join them
and then hurried from the Citadel along quiet streets
through gray predawn light. No other footprints disturbed the frost on the stones.

They rounded a corner, and a mist-shape floated
toward them. Responding instantly, Vank seared with
his light-weapon and it veered away. So the Graylord
had unloosed the grayvers, now that he no longer
feared the unknown powers of the Mage. The explosion would come barely in time.

Approaching the main gate, Shadow saw that the
portcullis had been raised and the entrance to Ad-
Omaq stood open. An Enforcer lay twisted on the
ground, his weapon still in its holster. Whether he
had been slain by one of her friends or by some
other desperate attacker made no difference.

After a scan with the clarity, the small band made
its way along an alley to where heaps of refuse had
been cleared aside and an old grating knocked askew,
releasing the dank foul smell of the sewers. Shadow
called, and Dorf ascended to meet them, halting
halfway through the opening at the sight of the Enforcers until Shadow told him what had happened.

The Mage's ghoul lay quietly in the arms of the
Enforcers, but it still breathed.

All that could be done now was to wait for Nle to
fire the fuses at the Citadel. Then would come Argen's
and Enra's blasts, and finally Dorf's.

Shadow moved to the mouth of the alley and looked up at the city. Its buildings loomed black against the awakening sky, a ray of dawn light turning the Citadel into a glowing column of pearl. Despite its beauty, this was a cruel city, degenerated from a learning center into a nest of tyrants and hedonists. Now even that was past. In the broad square before the gates, a sliver of mist wafted in through the shuttered window of a house and, moments later, out again.

The traces of sunlight faded as yellow-gray clouds blew in the from the sea, their lowering gloom adding to Shadow's disquiet. Dawn was upon them, almost past them, yet Nle hadn't fired his chain. He was first; they hadn't thought to make an alternate plan. Would Argen fire his powder? And where was Nle?

The first blast sounded like distant thunder, followed by a chain of booms shattering the hushed morning. Shutters flew wide and faces appeared at windows overhead, crying out in alarm. It wasn't Nle's blast, but Argen's, farther off, followed moments later by the shock of another series of explosions, from Enra's sector. The city was in turmoil. Highborns fled their houses in nightdress, city-sneaks pelted from alleys and corners, and over it all roiled the acrid pallor of smoke.

But the Citadel stood intact, and within it the storehouse containing the last great cache of powder, vital to bringing down the sewers. Had they destroyed so much of the city, only to leave the Radiants and the grayver-mold intact?

"I have to go back." Seeing Vank's confusion, Shadow added, "Nle was supposed to fire the Citadel."

At her words, the body of the Mage twisted sharply and, with sudden, superhuman strength, ripped apart the cords that bound its wrists and ankles. Wrenching free of the Enforcers, it staggered to its feet like a dropped marionette and lurched back toward the deadly white tower.

Without hesitation, Shadow and the Enforcers raced after it.

Chapter Twenty

In the winding streets, amid the panicked crowds, Shadow lost sight of Kirji. Vank and the other Enforcers pushed ahead, the people making way for them, then closing in. Kicking and shoving against the flow, Shadow fought her way toward the Citadel, expecting at any moment the vast imploding that would signal the doom of the Radiants, and Nle, and Kirji.

Someone caught her by the shoulder. Shadow struggled to free herself, then recognized Argen. He shouted over the noise of the mob. "Go back! I'm going to set it off myself."

"The Mage and Nle—they're in there!"

"It's too late! You've got to leave!" He tried to push her into the flow of the crowd surging toward the gates, but Shadow slipped away and ran on.

Outside the Citadel, where the great doors still stood open a crack, four Omaqi Enforcers and one from Kir lay slumped on the paving-stones, blackened wounds testifying to the nature of their battle.

Inside, the great hall resounded with silence after the clamor of the streets. A couple of servants scurried by, heads lowered. Yet it would not take the captain of the guard long to realize his makeshift defenses had been breached by armed Kirites.

At the foot of the stairs, Shadow paused. The clarity showed her that Vank and his men had gone upward, toward the Mage's chambers. But Kirji wasn't there.

From far below came the wail of a bloodcat. Briala and the Mage were with them, this much she could see. But with no sound to draw it, no place on which to focus, even the clarity couldn't find Nle.

Shadow owed the Mage nothing, as such things were measured in the underworld of Ad-Omaq. Nor would she throw her life away for him uselessly, as Mera had done for Taav. But Kirji and Shadow had touched each others' souls, and she knew instinctively that she would never be touched that way again. Between them lay bonds half-broken and they would bind her until death, or until the Mage, restored to himself, severed them of his own free choice.

Shadow descended to the fields. Even at this early hour, slaves toiled sullenly, row after row of them, many limping or marked by burns from the previous day. "Run!" Faces turned; rakes slowed. "To the forest! Now!"

She thought they would stand there forever, gaping at her like ring-babbles, and then they began to move, by ones and then in clumps, toward the stairs. Enforcers closed in on them. Someone yelled, and rakes and hoes clawed the air. As Shadow circled the barns, shrieks and hissing flames and the thud of feet cloaked her approach. She paused, hidden, afraid to use the clarity again. Instead, she edged around a shattered outbuilding, watching from the partial cover of jumbled boards.

Three figures stood above the bloodcats: Briala,

triumphant; the Mage, ghoul-empty; and—Shadow herself, startlingly real and bristling with defiance, as she had looked when she last confronted her half-sister in the prison. Briala had wasted no time in making use of the illusion-gift she'd taken along with Kirji's soul.

Briala grasped the Mage's arm and shoved him forward, toward the pit. The thing that had been Kirji walked numbly to the edge of death. Shadow wavered. To project the clarity here was surely to summon the Graylord, yet she must try to reach him.

But before she could act, the ghoul braced himself and stopped. His mouth formed a single syllable, "Kir." A blue anger glimmered through the whiteness as he turned toward Briala. It seemed to Shadow that in that moment he restored himself and would attack his tormentor, and then the tinge of selfhood ebbed and he folded to the ground.

Ignoring his body and the tumult from the fields, Briala stared across the pit at a thing of mist, huge and faintly luminous, tendrils of fog swirling inside its man-shape as it took form. The voice that spoke in Shadow's mind was deep, cruel, familiar. *So you have brought her*.

"Of course." Triumph lit Briala's yellow eyes as she gestured to the illusion-Shadow beside her. "You promised to allow me the pleasure of her capture; I have not failed you." Briala held out her arms. "And now I, too, am yours."

From where she stood motionless, Shadow watched the pair lock gazes across the pit. Something vaporish and white lifted from Briala and flew to the Graylord. Then the ghoul-Briala stepped forward, as if to follow her spirit, and dropped into the pit. From below came hideous tearing sounds.

A last figure waited on the bank, the illusion-Shadow. The mist-creature blew toward it, touched it, searched; stepping back toward safety, Shadow could feel the Graylord's confusion rising into fury. *She lied!*

Suddenly the jumble of boards no longer offered any protection. The Citadel, the city, the land of Omaq were too small to hide in.

The think felt her presence, growled within itself, and its fury abated. *So. You are here, after all.*

It had come to this: that she had escaped the caves of the Graylord, confounded the Mage's defenses, and mined the corrupt city so that it might be brought down, only to undo all that she had lived for because of her instinct to protect the Mage. Even now, Shadow did not begrudge him her life. But the clarity must not be allowed to fall to the Graylord.

A bloodcat keened, the body of its former mistress leaving its fierce appetite unsated. Death was no longer the enemy. Shadow leaped forward, determined to destroy herself before her gift could be taken.

A compulsion seized her to halt, turn aside, surrender herself. The same power with which the grayvers commanded in the mountains nearly held her. But she was stronger than before, and the clarity guided her. Moving forward was like fighting a rush of water, nearly drowning in the Omaq River, and then finding the air at last. As the frigid emptiness of the Graylord closed around her, Shadow plunged into the pit, tensing against a pain greater than human strength could endure.

And then, without warning, the earth began to

convulse. Someone—Nle or Argen—must have fired the blast-powder at last.

Walls roared forward; tons of rock and dirt thundered into the fields. The pit cleaved open. Bloodcats and Briala's torn body sprawled into the gap as spores and sewer muck blasted against Shadow's face.

Dirt filled her mouth. She choked, scrabbled, clawed, couldn't find the surface. There was no surface. There was nothing left anywhere but sludge and stones folding in upon themselves, crushing her lungs.

And then, suddenly, she felt hands grasp her and pull her free. Oh, blessed air! Gasping, Shadow managed at last to lift her head, and saw yellow eyes gazing at her. A Radiant.

"Is Briala dead?" the man demanded. She nodded weakly. "Thank the stars. I'm Yenat, Mera-ti; I was Briala's enemy, and her prisoner. Come."

"The Mage?"

"Here, what remains of him." As he spoke, the Radiant hoisted a slack form across his shoulders.

Her senses still clogged, Shadow stumbled and a russet-haired girl steadied her. "I'm Alea," she said. "I was Briala's prisoner, too."

"Come on," Yenat cut in. "We have to get out."

They clambered across a nightmare landscape of shifting boulders and yawning holes, the only light a flickering remnant of Radiant-magic from above. It reminded Shadow of an earlier time, in the Graylord's hall—where was the Graylord, in this blast-madness? And Nle; she hadn't found Nle.

Something else snared her thoughts. The storehouse. The great cache of powder. Through a welter of confusing images, the clarity found it. Intact. If it went off while they were still here . . .

Slaves and Enforcers jammed the stairs, their panicked shoving holding the mass at a standstill. Yenat flared light upward, bringing silence. "Calmly!" His words resonated. "There is no danger!" At Shadow's prompting, he added, "Go to the forest! To Kir for sanctuary!"

The crowd began to move and the three of them surged on, bolstering the heavily laden Yenat over the debris.

Somehow, eons later, they reached the ground level and the great hall, finding it less damaged but clogged with refugees. Radiants laden with gemstones lashed fire around in a futile effort to break through the mass of terrified slaves, while servants and Enforcers hauled sacks and pushed crates of stolen wealth, damming what few trickles of motion remained. It seemed as if the entire world was trying to fight its way through that one narrow opening in the great doors.

Shadow pressed to one side against the wall and edged around. With the skill of a city-sneak, she darted under an arm, between a pair of legs, over an obdurate figure until she found rough handholds and began to climb. Gaps scarred the wall, hindering her, but, propelled by desperation, she reached the controls, only to find the wheel still obdurate in her hands, even with all her strength thrown against it.

The platform creaked. Shadow sprang back, then recognized the wiry figure pulling up beside her. With a ghost of a smile, Nle put his shoulder to the task and together they wrestled the wheel until the gap widened below and the jam of bodies began to flow through.

"Why didn't you set off your powder?" she demanded when she could breathe freely again.

"I heard you'd been captured. I couldn't blow up the Citadel with you inside."

There was no time for further explanations. They scaled down near the doors, spying out Yenat with the Mage's body across his shoulders. Once outside, Nle led them at a shambling lope down twisted streets and alleyways, bypassing the teeming main roads. Even here, they were forced to thrust their way through the rabble and kick aside squealing munts and ring-babbles that had been frightened from their holes.

The surge of humanity, fodder for the mist-wraiths, was transmuting as it moved into ghouls that fell in turn upon their comrades. But there were too many people for the grayvers to take them all. And Radiants, for once finding their own needs meshed with the common good, torched many of the soulless victims and used the narrow-light to drive the grayvers back.

The mob fanned out across the great square, then funneled through the gates. The damage here was slight, evidence that Dorf had not yet fired his string. Highborns in rich costumes thronged alongside impoverished merchants with terrified eyes. Children cried for missing parents, and three figures staggered in chained terror, two Lost Women carrying a ghoul between them. Yenat parted them with the fire, and sent the white-eyed woman to her rest.

As Shadow reached the far edge of the square, the great cache of powder caught fire at last, shattering the Citadel in an explosion of light. Beneath her, the ground bucked and buildings spewed their stones onto the masses. The cries of the injured merged with the almost human groan of the sewers as they were ripped open by the terrible heaving of the earth.

The clarity, with its ever growing reach and power, showed her that the invading mold had been flung from its sanctum, exposed to the disabling power of even this thin daylight. Yet there remained, Shadow knew, the caverns in the mountains. While the mold from which he sprang flourished there, the Graylord surely still lived.

As they moved forward, Shadow searched the crowd for any more of her friends, but there were only Nle and Yenat, Alea and the body of Kirji. They passed over the Omaq River, its waters brown with offal, and into flatlands that had once been farms. Merchants, Highborns, slaves, and Radiants poured toward the east. Bolts of narrow-light continued to cull the ghouls and grayvers from among them, until only the people remained.

Kirji lay silent and slack across Yenat's shoulders, as if his ghoul-body, too, had died. But the blood still pulsed, if weakly. At last Shadow and her companions stopped on a rise to rest and wait for the others. From there, as the winter day darkened beneath a cloud of ashes, they watched the last charges crumple the gate. The city's mouth gaped open, broken-toothed.

Dorf and Enra reached them, and then Vank, the lone survivor of the Kirite Enforcers. Nothing more stirred in the city and the last of the line of refugees passed toward the forest. Argen did not come.

The sky was almost black by midday. Fearing a storm, they would have gone on, but the Mage was too weak. If he were not restored to himself now, it might be too late. With Vank's help, Shadow propped the Mage so she might look into his face.

At the movement, the hooded eyes opened dully.

Shadow's gaze met his. Her mind reached out, penetrating dimness and mist, white mist, a vast blankness. Something moved, faintly, then began to glow across the landscape of the void. Before she could take its measure, it gripped her, eyes locked into hers, wrenching her soul half out of her body. The world filled with harsh laughter.

In bringing Kirji, they had brought the Graylord as well.

Chapter Twenty-One

Now I have everything. After all these ages.

Not with her body could Shadow fight him, but with the clarity, which had become one with her soul. It was stronger now, yet for the first time since before Kir, she needed the strength of her comrades. Dorf knew and touched her. Other hands reached out—Enra, Nle, Alea, Vank, and finally Yenat. She felt the enemy waver.

If you won't come to me, I will come to you.

The force against her halted. Mist poured from the Mage's eyes, mouth, and ears, and shocked through Shadow's veins. Somewhere a body writhed, and people grasped it desperately. Whose body? Hers? The Graylord stunned her with his malevolence, blotting the warm edges of Shadowness, shrinking her soul to a wisp. Where was she? Whiteness, nothingness everywhere.

Briala. Briala was here, too. Shadow could feel her and Hakin. They had lost their life-forms, yet the sense of them was unmistakable.

As though recovering memory from the ancient past, Shadow let her mind go blank. The Graylord was trying to pull the clarity from her and now he couldn't find it. How could this be? Her spirit, Briala's, Hakin's, were all here, inside this body and this mist. And Kirji as well; Shadow sensed the writhing of his tormented being.

Escape is no longer possible. Come and be one with me.

The clarity brought her the Graylord's thoughts. Yet he couldn't hear hers. He was only another soul, like the rest; in control, but human. She hadn't known that until this moment. Only now did she see that he might be breached . . .

But in that instant the Graylord found her. His soul spread over hers, so that she saw how it had been deformed, distended with hatred and the power of centuries. Against it, drawing on the friends who somewhere still held her, she could offer only her own rough-edged gift.

Other things stirred, tatters of souls stolen down through the ages. There were perhaps a dozen; no, a hundred; more than that—thousands! They aligned themselves within the body of one girl, pitted against an evil so great it had achieved immortality.

You will never stand against me.

He had on his side time, long ages that had fed his savagery. She had only the clarity, and only one way to use it now, the deadliest path of all: to enter his mind.

First there was grayness, the grayver-mist that he had taken, when it would have taken him. Within that, ice-fire, burning white, a hunger to consume, a vast corrosive loathing of all that lived and drew breath; and yet before that, before he found the grayver-host, he had been a man.

There had been grayvers then, aimless things, taking humans who strayed within their caves—until a man came who let himself be swallowed, but instead of submitting he conquered. He made the mist shape itself to his ends, and grow, and burst out of the caves to spread across the earth. Shadow felt them around her, the lost of uncounted generations still helpless within their master.

Suddenly she felt a ripple in the fabric of the world. A new soul. Nle. He had left his body and entered hers, come to fight the final battle in this wasteland. And then the others joined her, all of them. Their fresh souls grappled with the overlord; yet the thing was winning. Strong with the spirits of its slaves, hardened by long practice, it drew their energy into itself. Alea was the first to weaken and yield; then the thing used her against them. The next to be absorbed was Vank, betrayed by his own divided loyalties.

Shadow's power ebbed. Slipping, grabbing for some nonexistent handhold of the mind, she tumbled toward the vortex. Lost, lost. . . .

Waves of light exploded against the forward momentum, breaking it. She felt the Graylord-spirit contort in agony. Whatever this cataclysm might be, it was tearing him apart.

With each wrench, souls spat out of the body amid dissolving mist. Shadow flew into the cold and then back in, restored to sole possession of her form. Around her, white tufts searched frantically for their shapes. A few, her friends, found them; the others, homeless, diffused at last. Somewhere among them must be Briala, and Hakin, and the man who had become the Graylord. Gone to wherever they should have gone long ago when their bodies died.

The chill outlines of the tangible world disoriented her, but at last Shadow distinguished a dull boom echoing from the hills. The clarity reached beyond itself to slag heaps that had been mountains, to caverns retching out their flickering mold, to crushed valleys that had once been home to the old race. The vistas of her childhood and the sneakways of her youth were both gone, blown to the far side of forever.

Now she understood. Lumle had spoken once of storing blast-powder on his ship, the same ship that was to anchor off the shores of Omaq and fetch him home after he delivered the Council's message to Briala. But he had not gone home. He had gone back to the mountains.

Something cold and white settled on her nose, a harmless snowflake. Or perhaps not so harmless. Three of her companions lay unmoving: Kirji, Vank, and Alea. Yenat knelt beside his lover and wept. But they weren't dead, not yet. They must be carried to shelter.

The small band took refuge in the same aging farmhouse where Shadow had once hidden. They were far from Kir and had no medicines to treat their injured. All they could do was to keep the room warm through the long hours of darkness and listen to the howling of the wind as it piled snow around the cabin.

In the morning, in the white stillness, dark figures moved toward them from the east. Enforcers, in the green uniforms of Kir, had come to bring their lord home.

Chapter Twenty-Two

After seeing that her companions were well settled in the palace at Ad-Kir, Shadow requested and was allowed to sleep in the Mage's chambers. She was accompanied in her vigil by his sister Fia and his first counselor, an old man who blamed himself for becoming sick on the journey to Ad-Omaq and failing to be at his lord's side.

In the days that followed, the other victims began to rouse, Alea tended by Yenat and Vank among his own family, but not the Mage. Healers came and examined their lord, placed strong herbs on the pillow and rubbed ointments into his skin.

On the fifth evening, Kirji stirred, mumbling indistinctly. The eyes opened at last, neither white nor turquoise any longer but a brooding forest green. He made an effort to speak. Shadow leaned closer.

He looked at her and said, "Briala?" Then, realizing, he turned away, and she knew that he was grieving for Briala's death.

The Mage remained ill for almost a month, attended at his request only by his counselors and his sister. As soon as he was pronounced well, he declared that he would travel to Ad-Son to confer with the Council.

Shadow had to see him, despite the pain it would cause her. On the day before his departure, she made her way to the garden.

She waited on a bench until the Mage was done speaking to a servant within, knowing he must have seen her approach. At last he came out, pale in the sunshine. He glanced at her as if seeing someone from the far reaches of memory, and waited for her to speak first.

"When you go to the Council, what will you say about my people?" She remained standing, formally.

Kirji stared at her directly for the first time. "You claim the right to rule Omaq?"

"Of course I do."

"You know nothing of ruling." He spoke without anger, almost wearily. "I must use my own judgment as to the best course."

"Don't you see, even now?" Shadow demanded. "It was interference from outside that nearly destroyed my country. The building of the Citadel itself was the Council's doing. It was they who separated the Radiants from the common people."

"Kir opposed that course," the Mage reminded her.

"But it wasn't Kir that saved us." Shadow wished they could sit together and talk quietly, but the closeness that had once warmed the air between them was gone. "Partly it was Lumle, but it would have done no good to blow up the mountains if the mold had triumphed inside the city. It was my gift from the land itself, the merging of the old race and the new, that saved us."

"The clarity?" Kirji shook his head. "You overestimate its effectiveness. And if the history of Omaq proves anything, it is that your people have no talent for governing themselves."

"That's not—"

He brushed past her attempt to speak. "We have enough untilled farmland in Kir to distribute among your peasants. The Radiants can work as artisans. Any others will have the same opportunities for training that we give our own citizens." He recited this speech as if he had rehearsed it. "In time, a plan can be made for the resettlement of Omaq, but there may still be traces of mold in the city. Grayvers were seen by the last to leave. We must blast what remains, before anyone can think of returning."

"I want nothing destroyed in Omaq, nothing, except with my consent!" Shadow felt the threads of her life pull together, as if Mera and Taav were standing beside her. This was the final battle, not against the grayvers but against Kir. "Each time I came in contact with the mold, the clarity intensified. If the mold increases our natural gifts, it may hold the key to the very discoveries you dream of, to help all our people. And in your ignorance, you would wipe it out!"

Kirji looked uncertain for the first time. "I never considered that the mold might have such value."

"Let me go with you to the Council."

"No." The answer was immediate and final. "My counselor admires you, but he has warned that you may have another motive in this. The Council agreed once to a marriage between your sister and me, with joint rule over the Eastern Lands, and if you ask it, they may again endorse a *regaja*. It is a poor system for governing a land. Such a partnership must be based on more than expediency."

A small bird fluttered and died in Shadow's heart. "Your counselor is mistaken. Omaq is mine by right. I would not sell my freedom to win it back from the Council. If I do choose a mate someday, it will be what you would call *farraja*, true marriage."

"I will tell the Council your views," Kirji said. The interview was at an end.

Shadow's friends joined her on the dock the next day to watch the Mage's ship depart. Around them, the crowd cheered, but the small knot of Omaqis stood silent.

Before the Council could hand down its decision, before her people could be scattered about Kir, Shadow would go back. She had only to glance into Nle's face, and Dorf's, and Yenat's, to know they would come with her.

Epilogue

Spring ploughing was under way by the time Lumle arrived at the new town of Peh-Maq, in the open plains between the mountains and the ruined city. He rode alone on a harthorn. The clarity had detected his coming even before he left his ship off the coast.

Shadow waited at the outskirts of the village to greet her old friend and to protect him, should any of the Omaqis respond with rage to whatever the Council had decided. No matter what news he brought, he was only the messenger; and in the end, it was she who had vanquished the Graylord.

Under the midday sun, she gazed at the farmers busily working in the fields, at the laborers erecting a town hall with Radiant-carved boards, and at the young women weaving and preparing food as they tended their children. It had been a hard winter. Before they left Kir, each Omaqi had sworn to fight the Council if necessary. But first they had had to survive the cold winds and the barrenness of the land. Their food was gone before the first thaw; only the clarity's ability to spy out munts and harkbirds had spared them the necessity of eating their precious cropseeds, and only the Radiant-made fires had kept them warm throughout the bitter nights. Even parts of the sea had crusted with ice, and so they had been spared the Council's decision until now.

Ahead, Lumle halted and lifted something from his pack. Sunlight sparkled from the amber bottle. He had brought finot.

Shadow guessed what it meant. Her smile and Lumle's answering one said enough: work halted in the fields, and gradually a shout of triumph went up, reaching into the village. Friends came running to hear the details of how the Council had acknowledged the sovereignty of Omaq, and admitted its own fault in establishing the Citadel five centuries ago. Further, the Council had ruled that the daughter of Mera and Taav should govern if it was the desire of the people; and so it was.

There was a celebration that afternoon among the free people of Omaq. Harthorns were slaughtered for a feast, and Highborn musicians played. The hardships were not ended, but for the space of a few hours they could be forgotten.

Not until evening, when she could speak with Lumle alone, did Shadow ask the question that troubled her. "What did the Mage tell the Council?"

"He made his proposal, that he should rule the Eastern Lands." Lumle puffed reflectively on his smoking-rod as they sat in Shadow's hut, before a snapping fire. "But to give him his due, the Mage presented your arguments as well. At times I thought he defended your position better than his own."

"Was he angry at their decision?"

"He agreed to accept you as Kir's equal in the Council, if you choose to join," said the messenger.

"And no, I wouldn't say he was angry. Almost relieved, to tell the truth."

It had already been decided, with the advice of Nle and Yenat, that Omaq should take its place at Ad-Son if the Council supported its independence, and Shadow told him this. Alea would be the first delegate, after her child was born in the summer.

Then, in answer to Lumle's questions, Shadow described the winter, and how a recovery party had ventured into the ruined city for tools and other goods, undisturbed by the few grayvers they saw.

Near the settlement, a harthorn had been found one morning with its throat torn out, but the clarity discovered no ghouls lingering in the area. Still, there was need for caution.

The next day, she showed Lumle the town: the rows of small sturdy houses; the hall that would serve as schoolroom and courthouse; and the hospital established by a Radiant who had lived for some time in Ad-Kir and studied with the doctors there. Already, the narrow-light had proved useful in surgery, and one man of the old race had demonstrated a talent for diagnosing ailments. Lumle promised to report these things to the Council.

But it was not these matters that impressed him most. As they walked, Shadow watched him study the Omaqis at work, Radiant and peasant, Highborn and Lost Woman together. The past was not forgotten —it was not in the way of humans to forget such things—but the people saw the need to accept each other, and they did.

That evening, preparing to leave early in the morning, Lumle gave Shadow a small parcel: a thin silver necklace from which dangled a round pendant of burnished Kir wood. It was a rare amulet, worked so that illusions would spring forth to frighten her enemies if she were ever in danger.

"I didn't know merchants sold such things." She held it to the light and felt power flowing within the wood.

"Nor do they." The messenger finished drinking his finot. "The Mage made it."

"For me?"

Lumle nodded. "The longer he reflects on what happened, the more truthfully he perceives it. I touched at Ad-Kir before coming here, and he asked me to give it to you."

She remembered Briala's eyes deepening with concentration as she confronted the Mage that first day in the great square. How much of her fascination for the Mage had been grayver-magic? Yet would his feelings for Briala have taken so long to dissipate, if they were not real?

The next day, Lumle departed. He said that someday he would return to Peh-Maq, when they had mastered the art of making finot. He wouldn't say where he was going next, only that it was on some mission of the Council, to a land not yet on the maps.

For some minutes after he passed out of sight, Shadow stared east toward the once-mysterious land of Kir. Part of her still walked the open streets of the harbor, still sat in the Mage's garden and inhaled his illusion-fragrances. Still loved him.

She fastened the smooth necklace about her throat and turned back to her people.

It was in the autumn, after the harvest but before the first snow, that the Mage rode to Peh-Maq, to make his peace with the ruler of Omaq.

There was a public ceremony, and music, and a modest exchange of gifts, for Shadow would accept no more than she could give. Her land was poor, she told the Mage, but in time it would be rich again. Already, the hospital impressed him.

On the second day, when they could speak privately, she thanked him for the necklace, which had routed a pack of ghouls that approached the village in late summer.

"It was little enough to give." He sat where Lumle had, in her plain hut. "I've tried these past months again and again to think of what I might say to you, but I feel so unworthy. You were my lover and my friend and saved my life when I had done you nothing but wrong."

"Did you love Briala?" she asked. "Do you still?"

"No, and no." A ruefulness touched his face, making it younger. "There's an old saying in Ad-Kir that I never understood till now: that a man is weakest where he is strong. I think I finally know what it means. My power is illusions, and so I never thought to look for them in anyone else. What I felt for Briala was my love for you, because she looked so much like you. She was shining and perfect, the way a young man dreams a woman will be before he knows that real luster comes only from knowing life with all its sorrows and renewals. And my ambition led me to deny that you were what you are, the natural heir to this land."

"I'm glad you didn't love her." Shadow put more wood on the fire, not because it burned low but because she felt the need to move.

"You said once that if you married, it would only be if you could have *farraja*," said the Mage. "A true marriage of the heart. Not a marriage of state."

She understood what he was asking. "I won't merge Omaq with any other land or accept any domination."

"Nor should you." He waited, his eyes shy with uncertainty.

"Then, yes," she said.

And so it came to be that the Mage of Kir was married in a small village in a land he did not rule, and all that winter foiled the darkness with illusions. And the Forest of Kir was ever thereafter kept open, and its paths were much traveled.

DAW
Creatures of Wonder

LAURIE J. MARKS
☐ **DELAN THE MISLAID** (UE2325—$3.95)
A misfit among a people not its own, Delan willingly goes away with the Walker Teksan to the Lowlands. But there, the Walker turns out to be a cruel master, a sorcerer who practices dark magic to keep Delan his slave—and who has diabolical plans to enslave Delan's people, the winged Aeyrie. And unless Delan can free itself from Teksan's spell, it may become the key to the ruin of its entire race.

☐ **MOONBANE MAGE** (UE2415—$3.95)
Here is the story of Delan's child, a spoiled royal progeny, who is kidnapped by an evil magician of its own species, and must tap reserves both personal and magical to save her race from a suicidal sorcerous war.

JACKIE HYMAN
☐ **SHADOWLIGHT** (UE2397—$3.50)
The Radiants have long ruled in the city of Ad-Omaq through their powers as adepts. Yet they are not the only magic wielders in the land. There is an older race, a horned people drawing strength from nature itself. To the Radiants, this race is a menace to be eliminated—but they have not counted on Shadow, born of both races and gifted with the special mind abilities of each. . . .

TAD WILLIAMS
☐ **TAILCHASER'S SONG** (UE2374—$4.95)
This best-selling feline fantasy epic tells the adventures of Fritti Tailchaser, a young ginger cat who sets out, with boundless enthusiasm, on a dangerous quest which leads him into the underground realm of an evil cat-god—a nightmare world from which only his own resources can deliver him.

DAW

Enter the Magical Worlds of

Tanya Huff

☐ **GATE OF DARKNESS, CIRCLE OF
LIGHT** (UE2386—$3.95)

The Wild Magic was loose in Toronto, for an Adept of Darkness had broken through the barrier into the everyday mortal world. And in this age when only fools and innocents still believed in magic, who was there to fight against this invasion by evil? But Toronto did have its unexpected champions of the Light: a street musician, a "simple" young girl, a bag lady, an overworked social worker, a streetwise cat, and Evan, Adept of Light, summoned to stand with these mortals in the ultimate war!

THE NOVELS OF CRYSTAL

☐ **CHILD OF THE GROVE: Book 1** (UE2432—$3.95)

Ardhan is a world slowly losing its magic. But one wizard still survives, a master of evil bent on world domination. No mere mortal can withstand him—and so the Elder Races must intervene. Their gift of hope to Ardhan is Crystal, the Child of the Grove, daughter of Power and the last-born wizard who will ever walk this world!

☐ **THE LAST WIZARD: Book 2** (UE2331—$3.95)

Kraydak, the evil sorcerer was dead, and Crystal's purpose for existing was gone. For in a world terrified of wizards, a land where only Lord Death was her friend, what future was there for Crystal, the last wizard ever to walk the world? Then she used her power to save a mortal's life and forged one final bond to humanity—a bond that would take her on a quest to destroy a long-dead wizard's stronghold of magic, a place which had lured many to their doom.

DAW

An Exciting New Fantasy Talent!

Mickey Zucker Reichert

THE BIFROST GUARDIANS